A FEARFUL RESPONSIBILITY

AND OTHER STORIES

BY

WILLIAM D. HOWELLS

AUTHOR OF "THE LADY OF THE AROOSTOOK," "THE UNDISCOVERED
COUNTRY," ETC.

GREENWOOD PRESS, PUBLISHERS
WESTPORT, CONNECTICUT

Originally published in 1884
by James R. Osgood and Company

First Greenwood Reprinting 1970

SBN 8371-2820-X

PRINTED IN UNITED STATES OF AMERICA

A FEARFUL RESPONSIBILITY.

CONTENTS.

A FEARFUL RESPONSIBILITY.

I.

EVERY loyal American who went abroad during the first years of our great war felt bound to make himself some excuse for turning his back on his country in the hour of her trouble. But when Owen Elmore sailed, no one else seemed to think that he needed excuse. All his friends said it was the best thing for him to do; that he could have leisure and quiet over there, and would be able to go on with his work.

At the risk of giving a farcical effect to my narrative, I am obliged to confess that the work of which Elmore's friends spoke was a projected history of Venice. So many literary Americans have projected such a work that it may now fairly be regarded as a national enterprise. Elmore was too obscure to have been announced in the usual way by the newspapers as having this design; but it was well known in his

town that he was collecting materials when his pro-
fessorship in the small inland college with which he
was connected lapsed through the enlistment of nearly
all the students.   The president became colonel of the
college regiment; and in parting with Elmore, while
their boys waited on the campus without, he had
said, "Now, Elmore, you must go on with your history of Venice.   Go to Venice and collect your materials on the spot.   We're coming through this all
right.   Mr. Seward puts it at sixty days, but I'll give
them six months to lay down their arms, and we shall
want you back at the end of the year.   Don't you
have any compunctions about going.   I know how
you feel; but it is perfectly right for you to keep out
of it.   Good-by."   They wrung each other's hands for
the last time,— the president fell at Fort Donelson;
but now Elmore followed him to the door, and when
he appeared there one of the boyish captains shouted,
"Three cheers for Professor Elmore!" and the president called for the tiger, and led it, whirling his cap
round his head.

Elmore went back to his study, sick at heart.   It
grieved and vexed him that even these had not
thought that he should go to the war, and that his
inward struggle on that point had been idle so far as
others were concerned.   He had been quite earnest

in the matter; he had once almost volunteered as
a private soldier: he had consulted his doctor, who
sternly discouraged him.   He would have been truly
glad of any accident that forced him into the ranks;
but, as he used afterward to say, it was not his idea
of soldiership to enlist for the hospital.   At the distance of five hundred miles from the scene of hostili-
ties, it was absurd to enter the Home Guard; and,
after all, there were, even at first, some selfish people
who went into the army, and some unselfish people
who kept out of it.   Elmore's bronchitis was a dis-
order which active service would undoubtedly have
aggravated; as it was, he made a last effort to be
of use to our Government as a bearer of dispatches.
Failing such an appointment, he submitted to expa-
triation as he best could; and in Italy he fought for
our cause against the English, whom he found everywhere all but in arms against us.

He sailed, in fine, with a very fair conscience.   " I
should be perfectly at ease," he said to his wife, as
the steamer dropped smoothly down to Sandy Hook,
"if I were sure that I was not glad to be getting
away."

"You are *not* glad," she answered.

"I don't know, I don't know," he said, with the
weak persistence of a man willing that his wife should

persuade him against his convictions; "I wish that I felt certain of it."

"You are too sick to go to the war; nobody expected you to go."

"I know that, and I can't say that I like it. As for being too sick, perhaps it's the part of a man to go if he dies on the way to the field. It would encourage the others," he added, smiling faintly.

She ignored the tint from Voltaire in replying: "Nonsense! It would do no good at all. At any rate, it's too late now."

"Yes, it's too late now."

The sea-sickness which shortly followed formed a diversion from his accusing thoughts. Each day of the voyage removed them further, and with the preoccupations of his first days in Europe, his travel to Italy, and his preparations for a long sojourn in Venice, they had softened to a pensive sense of self-sacrifice, which took a warmer or a cooler tinge according as the news from home was good or bad.

II.

HE lost no time in going to work in the Marcian Library, and he early applied to the Austrian authorities for leave to have transcripts made in the archives. The permission was negotiated by the American consul (then a young painter of the name of Ferris), who reported a mechanical facility on the part of the authorities, — as if, he said, they were used to obliging American historians of Venice. The foreign tyranny which cast a pathetic glamour over the romantic city had certainly not appeared to grudge such publicity as Elmore wished to give her heroic memories, though it was then at its most repressive period, and formed a check upon the whole life of the place. The tears were hardly yet dry in the despairing eyes that had seen the French fleet sail away from the Lido, after Solferino, without firing a shot in behalf of Venice; but Lombardy, the Duchies, the Sicilies, had all passed to Sardinia, and the Pope alone represented

the old order of native despotism in Italy.   At Venice
the Germans seemed tranquilly awaiting the change
which should destroy their system with the rest; and
in the meantime there had occurred one of those
impressive pauses, as notable in the lives of nations
as of men, when, after the occurrence of great events,
the forces of action and endurance seem to be gathering themselves against the stress of the future.   The
quiet was almost consciously a truce and not a peace ;
and this local calm had drawn into it certain elements
that picturesquely and sentimentally heightened the
charm of the place.   It was a refuge for many exiled
potentates and pretenders ; the gondolier pointed out
on the Grand Canal the palaces of the Count of Cham-
bord, the Duchess of Parma, and the Infante of Spain ;
and one met these fallen princes in the squares and
streets, bowing with distinct courtesy to any that
chose to salute them.   Every evening the Piazza San
Marco was filled with the white coats of the Austrian
officers, promenading to the exquisite military music
which has ceased there forever; the patrol clanked
through the footways at all hours of the night, and
the lagoon heard the cry of the sentinel from fort to
fort, and from gunboat to gunboat.   Through all this
the demonstration of the patriots went on, silent,
ceaseless, implacable, annulling every alien effort at

gayety, depopulating the theatres, and desolating the ancient holidays.

There was something very fine in this, as a spectacle, Elmore said to his young wife, and he had to admire the austere self-denial of a people who would not suffer their tyrants to see them happy; but they secretly owned to each other that it was fatiguing. Soon after coming to Venice they had made some acquaintance among the Italians through Mr. Ferris, and had early learned that the condition of knowing Venetians was not to know Austrians. It was easy and natural for them to submit, theoretically. As Americans, they must respond to any impulse for freedom, and certainly they could have no sympathy with such a system as that of Austria. By whatever was sacred in our own war upon slavery, they were bound to abhor oppression in every form. But it was hard to make the application of their hatred to the amiable-looking people whom they saw everywhere around them in the quality of tyrants, especially when their Venetian friends confessed that personally they liked the Austrians. Besides, if the whole truth must be told, they found that their friendship with the Italians was not always of the most penetrating sort, though it had a superficial intensity that for a while gave the effect of lasting cordiality. The Elmores were not quite able to decide whether the pause of feeling at which they arrived was through their own defect or not. Much was to be laid to the difference of race, religion, and education; but something, they feared, to the personal vapidity of acquaintances whose meridional liveliness made them yawn, and in whose society they did not always find compensation for the sacrifices they made for it.

"But it is right," said Elmore. "It would be a sort of treason to associate with the Austrians. We owe it to the Venetians to let them see that our feelings are with them."

"Yes," said his wife pensively.

"And it is better for us, as Americans abroad, during this war, to be retired."

"Well, we are retired," said Mrs. Elmore.

"Yes, there is no doubt of that," he returned.

They laughed, and made what they could of chance American acquaintances at the *caffès*. Elmore had his history to occupy him, and doubtless he could not understand how heavy the time hung upon his wife's hands. They went often to the theatre, and every evening they went to the Piazza, and ate an ice at Florian's. This was certainly amusement; and routine was so pleasant to his scholarly temperament that he enjoyed merely that.   He made a point of admitting his wife as much as possible into his intellectual life; he read her his notes as fast as he made them, and he consulted her upon the management of his theme, which, as his research extended, he found so vast that he was forced to decide upon a much lighter treatment than he had at first intended.   He had resolved upon a history which should be presented in a series of biograph- ical studies, and he was so much interested in this conclusion, and so charmed with the advantages of the form as they developed themselves, that he be- gan to lose the sense of social dulness, and ceased to imagine it in his wife.

A sort of indolence of the sensibilities, in fact, enabled him to endure *ennui* that made her frantic, and he was often deeply bored without knowing it at the time, or without a reasoned suffering.   He suffered as a child suffers, simply, almost ignorant- ly : it was upon reflection that his nerves began to quiver with retroactive anguish.   He was also able to idealize the situation when his wife no longer even wished to do so.   His fancy cast a poetry about these Venetian friends, whose conversation displayed the occasional sparkle of Ollendorff-English on a dark ground of lagoon-Italian, and whose vivid smiling

and gesticulation she wearied herself in hospitable
efforts to outdo. To his eyes their historic past
clothed them with its interest, and the long patience
of their hope and hatred under foreign rule enno-
bled them, while to hers they were too often only
tiresome visitors, whose powers of silence and of
eloquence were alike to be dreaded. It did not console her as it did her husband to reflect that they
probably bored the Italians as much in their turn.
When a young man, very sympathetic for literature
and the Americans, spent an evening, as it seemed to
her, in crying nothing but "Per Bácco!" she owned
that she liked better his oppressor, who once came by
chance, in the figure of a young lieutenant, and who
unbuckled his wife, as he called his sword, and, putting her in a corner, sat up on a chair in the middle
of the room and sang like a bird, and then told
ghost-stories. The songs were out of Heine, and
they reminded her of her girlish enthusiasm for
German. Elmore was troubled at the lieutenant's
visit, and feared it would cost them all their Italian friends; but she said boldly that she did not
care; and she never even tried to believe that the
life they saw in Venice was comparable to that of
their little college town at home, with its teas and
picnics, and simple, easy social gayeties. There she

had been a power in her way; she had entertained, and had helped to make some matches: but the Venetians ate nothing, and as for young people, they never saw each other but by stealth, and their matches were made by their parents on a money-basis. She could not adapt herself to this foreign life; it puzzled her, and her husband's conformity seemed to estrange them, as far as it went. It took away her spirit, and she grew listless and dull. Even the history began to lose its interest in her eyes; she doubted if the annals of such a people as she saw about her could ever be popular.

There were other things to make them melancholy in their exile. The war at home was going badly, where it was going at all. The letters now never spoke of any term to it; they expressed rather the dogged patience of the time when it seemed as if there could be no end, and indicated that the country had settled into shape about it, and was pushing forward its other affairs as if the war did not exist. Mrs. Elmore felt that the America which she had left had ceased to be. The letters were almost less a pleasure than a pain, but she always tore them open, and read them with eager unhappiness. There were miserable intervals of days and even weeks when no letters came, and when the Reuter telegrams in the Gazette of

Venice dribbled their vitriolic news of Northern disaster through a few words or lines, and Galignani's long columns were filled with the hostile exultation and prophecy of the London press.

III.

THEY had passed eighteen months of this sort of life in Venice when one day a letter dropped into it which sent a thousand ripples over its stagnant surface. Mrs. Elmore read it first to herself, with gasps and cries of pleasure and astonishment, which did not divert her husband from the perusal of some notes he had made the day before, and had brought to the breakfast-table with the intention of amusing her. When she flattened it out over his notes, and exacted his attention, he turned an unwilling and lack-lustre eye upon it; then he looked up at her.

"Did you expect she would come?" he asked, in ill-masked dismay.

"I don't suppose they had any idea of it at first. When Sue wrote me that Lily had been studying too hard, and had to be taken out of school, I said that I wished she could come over and pay us a visit. But I don't believe they dreamed of letting her — Sue says so — till the Mortons' coming seemed too good a chance to be lost. I am so glad of it, Owen! You know how much they have always done for me ; and here is a chance now to pay a little of it back."

"What in the world shall we do with her ? " he asked.

"Do ? Everything ! Why, Owen," she urged, with pathetic recognition of his coldness, "she is Susy Stevens's own sister ! "

"Oh, yes — yes," he admitted.

"And it was Susy who brought us together ! "

"Why, of course."

"And ought n't you to be glad of the opportunity ? "

"I *am* glad — *very* glad."

"It will be a relief to you instead of a care. She 's such a bright, intelligent girl that we can both sympathize with your work, and you won't have to go round with me all the time, and I can matronize her myself."

"I see, I see," Elmore replied, with scarcely abated seriousness. "Perhaps, if she is coming here for her health, she won't need much matronizing."

"Oh, pshaw! She 'll be well enough for *that !* She 's overdone a little at school. I shall take good care of her, I can tell you ; and I shall make her have a real good time. It 's quite flattering of Susy to trust her to us, so far away, and I shall write and tell her we both think so."

"Yes," said Elmore, "it's a fearful responsibility."

There are instances of the persistence of husbands in certain moods or points of view on which even wheedling has no effect. The wise woman perceives that in these cases she must trust entirely to the softening influences of time, and as much as possible she changes the subject; or if this is impossible she may hope something from presenting a still worse aspect of the affair. Mrs. Elmore said, in lifting the letter from the table: "If she sailed the 3d in the City of Timbuctoo, she will be at Queenstown on the 12th or 13th, and we shall have a letter from her by Wednesday saying when she will be at Genoa. That's as far as the Mortons can bring her, and there's where we must meet her."

"Meet her in Genoa! How?"

"By going there for her," replied Mrs. Elmore, as if this were the simplest thing in the world. "I have never seen Genoa."

Elmore now tacitly abandoned himself to his fate. His wife continued: "I need n't take anything. Merely run on, and right back."

"When must we go?" he asked.

"I don't know yet; but we shall have a letter to-morrow. Don't worry on my account, Owen. Her coming won't be a bit of care to me. It will give me something to do and to think about, and it will be a pleasure all the time to know that it's for Susy Stevens. And I shall like the companionship."

Elmore looked at his wife in surprise, for it had not occurred to him before that with his company she could desire any other companionship. He desired none but hers, and when he was about his work he often thought of her. He supposed that at these moments she thought of him, and found society, as he did, in such thoughts. But he was not a jealous or exacting man, and he said nothing. His treatment of the approaching visit from Susy Stevens's sister had not been enthusiastic, but a spark had kindled his imagination, and it burned warmer and brighter as the days went by. He found a charm in the thought of having this fresh young life here in his charge, and of teaching the girl to live into the great and beautiful history of the city: there was still much of the school-master in him, and he intended to make her sojourn an education to her; and as a literary man he hoped for novel effects from her mind upon material which he was above all trying to set in a new light before himself.

When the time had arrived for them to go and

meet Miss Mayhew at Genoa, he was more than re-
conciled to the necessity.   But at the last moment,
Mrs. Elmore had one of her old attacks.   What
these attacks were I find myself unable to specify,
but as every lady has an old attack of some kind,
I may safely leave their precise nature to conjecture.   It is enough that they were of a nervous
character, that they were accompanied with headache,
and that they prostrated her for several days.   During
their continuance she required the active sympathy
and constant presence of her husband, whose devotion was then exemplary, and brought up long arrears
of indebtedness in that way.

"Well, what shall we do?" he asked, as he sank
into a chair beside the lounge on which Mrs. Elmore
lay, her eyes closed, and a slice of lemon placed
on each of her throbbing temples with the effect of a
new sort of blinders.   "Shall I go alone for her?"

She gave his hand the kind of convulsive clutch
that signified, "Impossible for you to leave me."

He reflected.   "The Mortons will be pushing on
to Leghorn, and somebody *must* meet her.   How
would it do for Mr. Hoskins to go?"

Mrs. Elmore responded with a clutch tantamount
to "Horrors!   How could you think of such a
thing?"

"Well, then," he said, "the only thing we can do is to send a *valet de place* for her. We can send old Gazzi. He's the incarnation of respectability; five francs a day and his expenses will buy all the virtues of him. She'll come as safely with him as with me."

Mrs. Elmore had applied a vividly thoughtful pressure to her husband's hand; she now released it in token of assent, and he rose.

" But don't be gone long," she whispered.

On his way to the caffè which Gazzi frequented, Elmore fell in with the consul.

By this time a change had taken place in the consular office. Mr. Ferris, some months before, had suddenly thrown up his charge and gone home; and after the customary interval of ship-chandler, the California sculptor, Hoskins, had arrived out, with his commission in his pocket, and had set up his allegorical figure of The Pacific Slope in the room where Ferris had painted his too metaphysical conception of A Venetian Priest. Mrs. Elmore had never liked Ferris; she thought him cynical and opinionated, and she believed that he had not behaved quite well towards a young American lady, — a Miss Vervain, who had stayed awhile in Venice with her mother. She was glad to have him go; but she could not admire Mr. Hoskins, who, however good-hearted, was too hopelessly Western. He had had part of one foot shot away in the nine months' service, and walked with a limp that did him honor; and he knew as much of a consul's business as any of the authors or artists with whom it is the tradition to fill that office at Venice. Besides he was at least a fellow-American, and Elmore could not forbear telling him the trouble he was in : a young girl coming from their town in America as far as Genoa with friends, and expecting to be met there by the Elmores, with whom she was to pass some months ; Mrs. Elmore utterly prostrated by one of her old attacks, and he unable to leave her, or to take her with him to Genoa; the friends with whom Miss Mayhew travelled unable to bring her to Venice ; she, of course, unable to come alone. The case deepened and darkened in Elmore's view as he unfolded it.

"Why," cried the consul sympathetically, " if I could leave my post I 'd go ! "

"Oh, thank you ! " cried Elmore eagerly, remembering his wife. " I could n't think of letting you."

" Look here ! " said the consul, taking an official letter, with the seal broken, from his pocket. " This is the first time I could n't have left my post without distinct advantage to the public interests, since I 've been here. But with this letter from Turin, telling me to be on the lookout for the Alabama, I couldn't go to Genoa even to meet a young lady. The Austrians have never recognized the rebels as belligerents : if she enters the port of Venice, all I've got to do is to require the deposit of her papers with me, and then I should like to see her get out again. I *should* like to capture her. Of course, I don't mean Miss Mayhew," said the consul, recognizing the double sense in which his language could be taken.

" It would be a great thing for you," said Elmore, — " a *great* thing."

" Yes, it would set me up in my own eyes, and stop that infernal clatter inside about going over and taking a hand again."

" Yes," Elmore assented, with a twinge of the old shame. " I didn't know you had it too."

" If I could capture the Alabama, I could afford to let the other fellows fight it out."

" I congratulate you, with all my heart," said Elmore sadly, and he walked in silence beside the consul.

" Well," said the latter, with a laugh at Elmore's pensive rapture, " I'm as much obliged to you as if I *had* captured her. I'll go up to the Piazza with you, and see Gazzi."

The affair was easily arranged ; Gazzi was made

to feel by the consul's intervention that the shield of
American sovereignty had been extended over the
young girl whom he was to escort from Genoa, and
two days later he arrived with her. Mrs. Elmore's
attack now was passing off, and she was well enough
to receive Miss Mayhew half-recumbent on the sofa
where she had been prone till her arrival. It was
pretty to see her fond greeting of the girl, and her
joy in her presence as they sat down for the first long
talk; and Elmore realized, even in his dreamy withdrawal, how much the bright, active spirit of his wife
had suffered merely in the restriction of her English.
Now it was not only English they spoke, but that
American variety of the language of which I hope
we shall grow less and less ashamed; and not only
this, but their parlance was characterized by local
turns and accents, which all came welcomely back
to Mrs. Elmore, together with those still more intimate inflections which belonged to her own particular circle of friends in the little town of Patmos,
N. Y. Lily Mayhew was of course not of her own set,
being five or six years younger; but women, more
easily than men, ignore the disparities of age between
themselves and their juniors; and in Susy Stevens's
absence it seemed a sort of tribute to her to establish
her sister in the affection which Mrs. Elmore had so

long cherished. Their friendship had been of such a thoroughly trusted sort on both sides that Mrs. Stevens (the memorably brilliant Sue Mayhew in her girlish days) had felt perfectly free to act upon Mrs. Elmore's invitation to let Lily come out to her; and here the child was, as much at home as if she had just walked into Mrs. Elmore's parlor out of her sister's house in Patmos.

IV.

THEY briefly dispatched the facts relating to Miss Mayhew's voyage, and her journey to Genoa, and came as quickly as they could to all those things which Mrs. Elmore was thirsting to learn about the town and its people. " Is it much changed ? I suppose it is," she sighed. " The war changes everything."

"Oh, you don't notice the war much," said Miss Mayhew. " But Patmos *is* gay, — perfectly delightful. We 've got one of the camps there now; and *such* times as the girls have with the officers! We have lots of fun getting up things for the Sanitary. Hops on the parade-ground at the camp, and going out to see the prisoners, — you never saw such a place."

" The prisoners ? " murmured Mrs. Elmore.

"Why, *yes* !" cried Lily, with a gay laugh. " Did n't you know that we had a prison-camp too ? Some of the Southerners look real nice. I pitied them," she added, with unabated gayety.

"Your sister wrote to me," said Mrs. Elmore; "but I could n't realize it, I suppose, and so I forgot it."

"Yes," pursued Lily, "and Frank Halsey's in command. You would never know by the way he walks that he had a cork leg. Of course he can't dance, though, poor fellow. He's pale, and he's perfectly fascinating. So's Dick Burton, with his empty sleeve; he's one of the recruiting officers, and there's nobody so popular with the girls. You can't think how funny it is, Professor Elmore, to see the old college buildings used for barracks. Dick says it's much livelier than it was when he was a student there."

"I suppose it must be," dreamily assented the professor. "Does he find plenty of volunteers?"

"Well, you know," the young girl explained, "that the old style of volunteering is all over."

"No, I did n't know it."

"Yes. It's the bounties now that they rely upon, and they do say that it will come to the draft very soon, now. Some of the young men have gone to Canada. But everybody despises *them*. Oh, Mrs. Elmore, I should think you'd be *so* glad to have the professor off here, and honorably out of the way!"

"I'm *dis*honorably out of the way; I can never forgive myself for not going to the war," said Elmore.

"Why, how ridiculous!" cried Lily. "Nobody feels that way about it *now!* As Dick Burton says, we've come down to business. I tell you, when you see arms and legs off in every direction, and women going about in black, you don't feel that it's such a romantic thing any more. There are mighty few engagements now, Mrs. Elmore, when a regiment sets off; no presentation of revolvers in the town hall; and some of the widows have got married again; and that I don't think *is* right. But what can they do, poor things? You remember Tom Friar's widow, Mrs. Elmore?"

"Tom Friar's *widow!* Is Tom Friar *dead?*"

"Why, of course! One of the first. I think it was Ball's Bluff. Well, *she's* married. But she married his cousin, and as Dick Burton says, that isn't so bad. Isn't it awful, Mrs. Clapp's losing *all* her boys, — all five of them? It does seem to bear too hard on *some* families. And then, when you see every one of those six Armstrongs going through without a scratch!"

"I suppose," said Elmore, "that business is at a standstill. The streets must look rather dreary."

"*Business* at a standstill!" exclaimed Lily. "What *has* Sue been writing you all this time? Why, there never was such prosperity in Patmos before! Every-

body is making money, and people that you would n't
hardly speak to a year ago are giving parties and in-
viting the old college families.   You ought to see the
residences and business blocks going up all over the
place.   I don't suppose you would know Patmos now.
You remember George Fenton, Mrs. Elmore ? "

" Mr. Haskell's clerk ? "

" Yes.   Well, he 's made a fortune out of an
army contract; and he 's going to marry — the
engagement came out just before I left — Bella
Stearns."

At these words Mrs. Elmore sat upright, — the
only posture in which the fact could be imagined.
" Lily ! "

" Oh, I can tell you these are gay times in America," triumphed the young girl.   She now put her
hand to her mouth and hid a yawn.

" You 're sleepy," said Mrs. Elmore.   " Well, you
know the way to your room.   You 'll find everything
ready there, and I shall let you go alone.   You shall
commence being at home at once."

" Yes, I *am* sleepy," assented Lily ; and she promptly
said her good-nights and vanished ; though a keener
eye than Elmore's might have seen that her prompt-
ness had a color — or say light — of hesitation in it.

But he only walked up and down the room, after

she was gone, in unheedful distress. "Gay times in America! Good heavens! Is the child utterly heartless, Celia, or is she merely obtuse?"

"She certainly is n't at all like Sue," sighed Mrs. Elmore, who had not had time to formulate Lily's defence. "But she 's excited now, and a little off her balance. She 'll be different to-morrow. Besides, all America seems changed, and the people with it. We should n't have noticed it if we had stayed there, but we feel it after this absence."

"I never realized it before, as I did from her babble! The letters have told us the same thing, but they were like the histories of other times. Camps, prisoners, barracks, mutilation, widowhood, death, sudden gains, social upheavals, — it is the old, hideous story of war come true of our day and country. It 's terrible!"

"She will miss the excitement," said Mrs. Elmore. "I don't know exactly what we shall do with her. Of course, she can't expect the attentions she 's been used to in Patmos, with those young men."

Elmore stopped, and stared at his wife. "What do you mean, Celia?"

"We don't go into society at all, and she does n't speak Italian. How shall we amuse her?"

"Well, upon my word, I don't know that we 're

obliged to provide her amusement! Let her amuse herself. Let her take up some branch of study, or of — of — research, and get something besides 'fun' into her head, if possible." He spoke boldly, but his wife's question had unnerved him, for he had a soft heart, and liked people about him to be happy. "We can show her the objects of interest. And there are the theatres," he added.

"Yes, that is true," said Mrs. Elmore. "We can both go about with her. I will just peep in at her now, and see if she has everything she wants." She rose from her sofa and went to Lily's room, whence she did not return for nearly three quarters of an hour. By this time Elmore had got out his notes, and, in their transcription and classification, had fallen into forgetfulness of his troubles. His wife closed the door behind her, and said in a low voice, little above a whisper, as she sank very quietly into a chair, "Well, it has all come out, Owen."

"What has all come out?" he asked, looking up stupidly.

"I knew that she had something on her mind, by the way she acted. And you saw her give me that look as she went out?"

"No — no, I did n't. What look was it? She looked sleepy."

"She looked terribly, terribly excited, and as if she would like to say something to me. That was the reason I said I would let her go to her room alone."

" Oh ! "

" Of course she would have felt awfully if I had gone straight off with her. So I waited. It *may* never come to anything in the world, and I don't suppose it will ; but it 's quite enough to account for everything you saw in her."

" I did n't see anything in her, — that was the difficulty. But what is it — what is it, Celia ? You know how I hate these delays."

" Why, I 'm not sure that I need tell you, Owen ; and yet I suppose I had better. It will be safer," said Mrs. Elmore, nursing her mystery to the last, enjoying it for its own sake, and dreading it for its effect upon her husband. " I suppose you will think your troubles are beginning pretty early," she suggested.

" Is it a trouble ? "

" Well, I don't know that it is. If it comes to the very worst, I dare say that every one would n't call it a trouble."

Elmore threw himself back in his chair in an attitude of endurance. " What would the worst be ? "

"Why, it's no use even to discuss that, for it's perfectly absurd to suppose that it could ever come to that. But the case," added Mrs. Elmore, perceiving that further delay was only further suffering for her husband, and that any fact would now probably fall far short of his apprehensions, "is simply this, and I don't know that it amounts to anything; but at Peschiera, just before the train started, she looked out of the window, and saw a splendid officer walking up and down and smoking; and before she could draw back he must have seen her, for he threw away his cigar instantly, and got into the same compartment. He talked awhile in German with an old gentleman who was there, and then he spoke in Italian with Gazzi; and afterwards, when he heard her speaking English with Gazzi, he joined in. I don't know how he came to join in at first, and she does n't, either; but it seems that he knew some English, and he began speaking. He was very tall and handsome and distinguished-looking, and a *perfect* gentleman in his manners; and she says that she saw Gazzi looking rather queer, but he did n't say anything, and so she kept on talking. She told him at once that she was an American, and that she was coming here to stay with friends; and, as he was very curious about America, she told him all she

could think of. It did her good to talk about home,
for she had been feeling a little blue at being so far
away from everybody. Now, *I* don't see any harm
in it; do you, Owen ? "

"It is n't according to the custom here; but we
need n't care for that. Of course it was imprudent."

"Of course," Mrs. Elmore admitted. "The officer
was very polite; and when he found that she was
from America, it turned out that he was a *great*
sympathizer with the North, and that he had a
brother in our army. Don't you think that was
nice ? "

"Probably some mere soldier of fortune, with no
heart in the cause," said Elmore.

"And very likely he has no brother there, as I told
Lily. He told her he was coming to Padua; but
when they reached Padua, he came right on to Venice.
That *shows* you could n't place any dependence upon
what he said. He said he expected to be put under
arrest for it; but he did n't care, — he was coming.
Do you believe they 'll put him under arrest ? "

"I don't know — I don 't know," said Elmore, in a
voice of grief and apprehension, which might well
have seemed anxiety for the officer's liberty.

"I told her it was one of his jokes. He was very
funny, and kept her laughing the whole way, with

his broken English and his witty little remarks. She says he's just dying to go to America. Who do you suppose it can be, Owen?"

"How should I know? We've no acquaintance among the Austrians," groaned Elmore.

"That's what I told Lily. She's no idea of the state of things here, and she was quite horrified. But she says he was a perfect gentleman in everything. He belongs to the engineer corps, — that's one of the highest branches of the service, he told her, — and he gave her his card."

"Gave her his card!"

Mrs. Elmore had it in the hand which she had been keeping in her pocket, and she now suddenly produced it; and Elmore read the name and address of Ernst von Ehrhardt, Captain of the Royal-Imperial Engineers, Peschiera. "She says she knows he wanted hers, but she didn't offer to give it to him; and he didn't ask her where she was going, or anything."

"He knew that he could get her address from Gazzi for ten soldi as soon as her back was turned," said Elmore cynically. "What then?"

"Why, he said — and this is the only really bold thing he *did* do — that he must see her again, and that he should stay over a day in Venice in hopes of meeting her at the theatre or somewhere."

"It's a piece of high-handed impudence!" cried Elmore. "Now, Celia, you see what these people are! Do you wonder that the Italians hate them?"

"You've often said they only hate their system."

"The Austrians are part of their system. He thinks he can take any liberty with us because he is an Austrian officer! Lily must not stir out of the house to-morrow."

"She will be too tired to do so," said Mrs. Elmore.

"And if he molests us further, I will appeal to the consul." Elmore began to walk up and down the room again.

"Well, I don't know whether you could call it *molesting*, exactly," suggested Mrs. Elmore.

"What do you mean, Celia? Do you suppose that she — she — encouraged this officer?"

"Owen! It was all in the simplicity and innocence of her heart!"

"Well, then, that she wishes to see him again?"

"Certainly not! But that's no reason why we should be rude about it."

"Rude about it? How? Is simply avoiding him rudeness? Is proposing to protect ourselves from his impertinence rudeness?"

"No. And if you can't see the matter for yourself, Owen, I don't know how any one is to make you."

"Why, Celia, one would think that you approved of this man's behavior, — that *you* wished her to meet him again! You understand what the consequences would be if we received this officer. You know how all the Venetians would drop us, and we should have no acquaintances here outside of the army."

"Who has asked you to receive him, Owen? And as for the Italians dropping us, that does n't frighten me. But what could he do if he did meet her again? She need n't look at him. She says he is very intelligent, and that he has read a great many English books, though he does n't speak it very well, and that he knows more about the war than she does. But of course she won't go out to-morrow. All that I hate is that we should seem to be frightened into staying at home."

"She need n't stay in on his account. You said she would be too tired to go out."

"I see by the scattering way you talk, Owen, that your mind is n't on the subject, and that you 're anxious to get back to your work. I won't keep you."

"Celia, Celia! Be fair, now!" cried Elmore. "You know very well that I 'm only too deeply interested in this matter, and that I 'm not likely to get back to my work to-night, at least. What is it you wish me to do?"

Mrs. Elmore considered a while. "I don't wish you to do anything," she returned placably. "Of course, you're perfectly right in not choosing to let an acquaintance begun in that way go any further. We should n't at home, and we sha'n't here. But I don't wish you to think that Lily has been imprudent, under the circumstances. She does n't know that it was anything out of the way, but she happened to do the best that any one could. Of course, it was very exciting and very romantic; girls like such things, and there's no reason they should n't. We must manage," added Mrs. Elmore, "so that she shall see that we appreciate her conduct, and trust in her entirely. I would n't do anything to wound her pride or self-confidence. I would rather send her out alone to-morrow."

"Of course," said Elmore.

"And if I were with her when she met him, I believe I should leave it entirely to her how to behave."

"Well," said Elmore, "you're not likely to be put to the test. He'll hardly force his way into the house, and she is n't going out."

"No," said Mrs. Elmore. She added, after a silence,

"I'm trying to think whether I've ever seen him in Venice; he's here often. But there are so many tall officers with fair complexions and English beards. I *should* like to know how he looks! She said he was very aristocratic-looking."

"Yes, it's a fine type," said Elmore. "They're all nobles, I believe."

"But after all, they're no better looking than our boys, who come up out of nothing."

"Ours are Americans," said Elmore.

"And they are the best husbands, as I told Lily."

Elmore looked at his wife, as she turned dreamily to leave the room; but since the conversation had taken this impersonal turn he would not say anything to change its complexion. A conjecture vaguely taking shape in his mind resolved itself to nothing again, and left him with only the ache of something unascertained.

V.

In the morning Lily came to breakfast as bloom-
ing as a rose. The sense of her simple, fresh, whole-
some loveliness might have pierced even the indifference of a man to whom there was but one pretty
woman in the world, and who had lived since their
marriage as if his wife had absorbed her whole sex
into herself : this deep, unconscious constancy was a
noble trait in him, but it is not so rare in men as
women would have us believe. For Elmore, Miss
Mayhew merely pervaded the place in her finer
way, as the flowers on the table did, as the sweet
butter, the new eggs, and the morning's French
bread did ; he looked at her with a perfectly serene
ignorance of her piquant face, her beautiful eyes
and abundant hair, and her trim, straight figure.
But his wife exulted in every particular of her
charm, and was as generously glad of it as if it were
her own ; as women are when they are sure that the
charm of others has no designs. The ladies twit-

tered and laughed together, and as he was a man
without small talk, he soon dropped out of the conversation into a reverie, from which he found himself
presently extracted by a question from his wife.

"We had better go in a gondola, had n't we,
Owen?" She seemed to be, as she put this, trying
to look something into him. He, on his part, tried
his best to make out her meaning but failed.

He simply asked, "Where? Are you going out?"

"Yes. Lily has some shopping she *must* do. I
think we can get it at Pazienti's in San Polo."

Again she tried to pierce him with her meaning.
It seemed to him a sudden advance from the position
she had taken the night before in regard to Miss
Mayhew's not going out; but he could not understand
his wife's look, and he feared to misinterpret if he
opposed her going. He decided that she wished him
for some reason to oppose the gondola, so he said,
"I think you 'd better walk, if Lily is n't too tired."

"Oh, *I' m* not tired at all!" she cried.

"I can go with you, in that direction, on my way
to the library," he added.

"Well, that will be very nice," said Mrs. Elmore,
discontinuing her look, and leaving her husband
with an uneasy sense of wantonly assumed responsibility.

"She can step into the Frari a moment, and see those tombs," he said. "I think it will amuse her."

Lily broke into a laugh. "Is that the way you amuse yourselves in Venice?" she asked; and Mrs. Elmore hastened to reassure her.

"That's the way Mr. Elmore amuses himself. You know his history makes every bit of the past fascinating to him."

"Oh, yes, that history! Everybody is looking out for that," said Lily.

"Is it possible," said Elmore, with a pensive sarcasm in which an agreeable sense of flattery lurked, "that people still remember me and my history?"

"Yes, indeed!" cried Miss Mayhew. "Frank Halsey was talking about it the night before I left. He couldn't seem to understand why I should be coming to you at Venice, because he said it was a history of Florence you were writing. It isn't, is it? You must be getting pretty near the end of it, Professor Elmore."

"I'm getting pretty near the beginning," said Elmore sadly.

"It must be hard writing histories; they're so awfully hard to read," said Lily innocently. "Does it interest you?" she asked, with unaffected compassion.

"Yes," he said, "far more than it will ever interest anybody else."

"Oh, I don't believe that!" she cried sweetly, seizing the occasion to get in a little compliment.

Mrs. Elmore sat silent, while things were thus going against Miss Mayhew, and perhaps she was then meditating the stroke by which she restored the balance to her own favor as soon as she saw her husband alone after breakfast. "Well, Owen," she said, "you've done it now."

"Done what?" he demanded.

"Oh, nothing, perhaps!" she answered, while she got on her things for the walk with unusual gayety; and, with the consciousness of unknown guilt depressing him, he followed the ladies upon their errand, subdued, distraught, but gradually forgetting his sin, as he forgot everything but his history. His wife hated to see him so miserable, and whispered at the shop-door where they parted, "Don't be troubled, Owen! I didn't mean anything."

"By what?"

"Oh, if you've forgotten, never mind!" she cried; and she and Miss Mayhew disappeared within.

It was two hours later when he next saw them, after he had turned over the book he wished to see, and had found the passage which would enable him to go on with his work for the rest of the day at home. He was fitting his key into the house-door when he happened to look up the little street toward the bridge that led into it, and there, defined against the sky on the level of the bridge, he saw Mrs. Elmore and Miss Mayhew receiving the adieux of a distinguished-looking man in the Austrian uniform. The officer had brought his heels together in the conventional manner, and with his cap in his right hand, while his left rested on the hilt of his sword, and pressed it down, he was bowing from the hips. Once, twice, and he was gone.

The ladies came down the *calle* with rapid steps and flushed faces, and Elmore let them in. His wife whispered as she brushed by his elbow, "I want to speak with you instantly, Owen. Well, now!" she added, when they were alone in their own room and she had shut the door, "what do you say *now?*"

"What do *I* say now, Celia?" retorted Elmore, with just indignation. "It seems to me that it is for *you* to say something — or nothing."

"Why, you brought it on us."

Elmore merely glanced at his wife, and did not speak, for this passed all force of language.

"Did n't you see me looking at you when I spoke of going out in a gondola, at breakfast?"

"Yes."

"What did you suppose I meant?"

" I did n't know."

" When I was trying to make you understand that if we took a gondola we could go and come without being seen ! Lily *had* to do her shopping. But if you chose to run off on some interpretation of your own, was *I* to blame, I should like to know ? No, indeed ! You won't get me to admit it, Owen."

Elmore continued inarticulate, but he made a low, miserable sibillation between his set teeth.

" Such presumption, such perfect audacity I never saw in my life!" cried Mrs. Elmore, fleetly changing the subject in her own mind, and leaving her husband to follow her as he could. "It was outrageous!" Her words were strong, but she did not really look affronted ; and it is hard to tell what sort of liberty it is that affronts a woman. It seems to depend a great deal upon the person who takes the liberty.

" That was the man, I suppose," said Elmore quietly.

" Yes, Owen," answered his wife, with beautiful candor, " it was." Seeing that he remained unaffected by her display of this virtue, she added, " Don't you think he was very handsome ? "

" I could n't judge, at such a distance."

" Well, he is perfectly splendid. And I don't want you to think he was disrespectful at all. He was n't.

He was everything that was delicate and deferential."

"Did you ask him to walk home with you?"

Mrs. Elmore remained speechless for some moments. Then she drew a long breath, and said firmly: "If you won't interrupt me with gratuitous insults, Owen, I will tell you all about it, and then perhaps you will be ready to do me *justice*. I ask nothing more." She waited for his contrition, but proceeded without it, in a somewhat meeker strain: "Lily could n't get her things at Pazienti's, and we had to go to the Merceria for them. Then of course the nearest way home was through St. Mark's Square. I made Lily go on the Florian side, so as to avoid the officers who were sitting at the Quadri, and we had got through the square and past San Moïsè, as far as the Stadt Gratz. I had never thought of how the officers frequented the Stadt Gratz, but there we met a most magnificent creature, and I had just said, 'What a splendid officer!' when she gave a sort of stop and he gave a sort of stop, and bowed very low, and she whispered, 'It's my officer.' I did n't dream of his joining us, and I don't think he did, at first; but after he took a second look at Lily, it really seemed as if he could n't help it. He asked if he might join us, and I did n't say anything."

"Did n't say anything!"

"*No!* How could I refuse, in so many words? And I was frightened and confused, any way. He asked if we were going to the music in the Giardini Pubblici; and I said No, that Miss Mayhew was not going into society in Venice, but was merely here for her health. That's all there is of it. Now do you blame me, Owen?"

"No."

"Do you blame her?"

"No."

"Well, I don't see how *he* was to blame."

"The transaction was a little irregular, but it was highly creditable to all parties concerned."

Mrs. Elmore grew still meeker under this irony. Indignation and censure she would have known how to meet; but his quiet perplexed her: she did not know what might not be coming. "Lily scarcely spoke to him," she pursued, "and I was very cold. I spoke to him in German."

"Is German a particularly repellent tongue?"

"No. But I was determined he should get no hold upon us. He was very polite and very respectful, as I said, but I did n't give him an atom of encouragement; I saw that he was dying to be asked to call, but I parted from him very stiffly."

"Is it possible?"

"Owen, what *is* there so wrong about it all? He's clearly fascinated with her; and as the matter stood, he had no hope of seeing her or speaking with her except on the street. Perhaps he did n't know it was wrong, — or did n't realize it."

"I dare say."

"What else could the poor fellow have done? There he was! He had stayed over a day, and laid himself open to arrest, on the bare chance — one in a hundred — of seeing Lily; and when he did see her, what was he to do?"

"Obviously, to join her and walk home with her."

"You are too bad, Owen! Suppose it had been one of our own poor boys? He *looked* like an American."

"He did n't behave like one. One of 'our own poor boys,' as you call them, would have been as far as possible from thrusting himself upon you. He would have had too much reverence for you, too much self-respect, too much pride."

"What has pride to do with such things, my dear? I think he acted very naturally. He acted upon impulse. I 'm sure you 're always crying out against the restraints and conventionalities between young people, over here; and now, when a European *does* do a simple, unaffected thing — "

Elmore made a gesture of impatience. " This fellow has presumed upon your being Americans — on your ignorance of the customs here — to take a liberty that he would not have dreamed of taking with Italian or German ladies. He has shown himself no gentleman."

"Now there you are very much mistaken, Owen. That's what I thought when Lily first told me about his speaking to her in the cars, and I was very much prejudiced against him; but when I saw him to-day, I must say that I felt that I had been wrong. He *is* a gentleman ; but — he is desperate."

" Oh, indeed !"

"Yes," said Mrs. Elmore, shrinking a little under her husband's sarcastic tone. "Why, Owen," she pleaded, " can't you see anything romantic in it ?"

"I see nothing but a vulgar impertinence in it. I see it from his standpoint as an adventure, to be bragged of and laughed over at the mess-table and the caffè. I'm going to put a stop to it."

Mrs. Elmore looked daunted and a little bewildered. "Well, Owen," she said, "I put the affair entirely in your hands."

Elmore never could decide upon just what theory his wife had acted; he had to rest upon the fact, already known to him, of her perfect truth and conscientiousness, and his perception that even in a good woman the passion for manœuvring and intrigue may approach the point at which men commit forgery. He now saw her quelled and submissive; but he was by no means sure that she looked at the affair as he did, or that she voluntarily acquiesced.

"All that I ask is that you won't do anything that you 'll regret afterward. And as for putting a stop to it, I fancy it 's put a stop to already. He 's going back to Peschiera this afternoon, and that 'll probably be the last of him."

"Very well," said Elmore, "if that is the last of him, I ask nothing better. I certainly have no wish to take any steps in the matter."

But he went out of the house very unhappy and greatly perplexed. He thought at first of going to the Stadt Gratz, where Captain Ehrhardt was probably staying for the tap of Vienna beer peculiar to that hostelry, and of inquiring him out, and requesting him to discontinue his attentions; but this course, upon reflection, was less high-handed than comported with his present mood, and he turned aside to seek advice of his consul. He found Mr. Hoskins in the best humor for backing his quarrel. He had just received a second dispatch from Turin, stating that the rumor of the approaching visit of

the Alabama was unfounded; and he was thus left
with a force of unexpended belligerence on his hands
which he was glad to contribute to the defence of
Mr. Elmore's family from the pursuit of this Austrian officer.

" This is a very simple affair, Mr. Elmore," — he usually said " Elmore," but in his haughty frame of mind,
he naturally threw something more of state into their
intercourse, — " a very simple affair, fortunately.   All
that I have to do is to call on the military governor,
and state the facts of the case, and this fellow will
get his orders quietly and *definitively*.   This war has
sapped our influence in Europe, — there's no doubt of
it; but I think it's a pity if an American family liv-
ing in this city can't be safe from molestation; and
if it can't, I want to know the reason why."

This language was very acceptable to Elmore, and
he thanked the consul.   At the same time he felt his
own resentment moderated, and he said, " I 'm willing
to let the matter rest if he goes away this afternoon."

"Oh, of course," Hoskins assented, "if he clears
out, that's the end of it.   I 'll look in to-morrow,
and see how you 're getting along."

"Don't — don't give them the impression that
I 've — profited by your kindness," suggested Elmore
at parting.

"You haven't yet. I only hope you may have the chance."

"Thank you; I don't think *I* do."

Elmore took a long walk, and returned home tranquillized and clarified as to the situation. Since it could be terminated without difficulty and without scandal in the way Hoskins had explained, he was not unwilling to see a certain poetry in it. He could not repress a degree of sympathy with the bold young fellow who had overstepped the conventional proprieties in the ardor of a romantic impulse, and he could see how this very boldness, while it had a terror, would have a charm for a young girl. There was no necessity, except for the purpose of holding Mrs. Elmore in check, to look at it in an ugly light. Perhaps the officer had inferred from Lily's innocent frankness of manner that this sort of approach was permissible with Americans, and was not amusing himself with the adventure, but was in love in earnest. Elmore could allow himself this view of a case which he had so completely in his own hands; and he was sensible of a sort of pleasure in the novel responsibility thrown upon him. Few men at his age were called upon to stand in the place of a parent to a young girl, to intervene in her affairs, and to decide who was and who was not a proper person to pretend to her acquaintance.

Feeling so secure in his right, he rebelled against the restraint he had proposed to himself, and at dinner he invited the ladies to go to the opera with him. He chose to show himself in public with them, and to check any impression that they were without due protection. As usual, the pit was full of officers, and between the acts they all rose, as usual, and faced the boxes, which they perused through their *lorgnettes* till the bell rang for the curtain to rise. But Mrs. Elmore, having touched his arm to attract his notice, instructed him, by a slow turning of her head, that Captain Ehrhardt was not there. After that he undoubtedly breathed freer, and, in the relaxation from his sense of bravado, he enjoyed the last acts of the opera more than the first. Miss Mayhew showed no disappointment; and she bore herself with so much grace and dignity, and yet so evidently impressed every one with her beauty, that he was proud of having her in charge. He began himself to see that she was pretty.

VI.

THE next day was Sunday, and in going to church they missed a call from Hoskins, whom Elmore felt bound to visit the following morning on his way to the library, and inform of his belief that the enemy had quitted Venice, and that the whole affair was probably at an end. He was strengthened in this opinion by Mrs. Elmore's fear that she might have been colder than she supposed; she hoped that she had not hurt the poor young fellow's feelings; and now that he was gone, and safely out of the way, Elmore hoped so too.

On his return from the library, his wife met him with an air of mystery before which his heart sank. " Owen," she said, " Lily has a letter."

" Not bad news from home, Celia ! "

" No ; a letter which she wishes to show you. It has just come. As I don't wish to influence you, I would rather not be present." Mrs. Elmore slipped out of the room, and Miss Mayhew glided gravely in, holding an open note in her hand, and looking into Elmore's eyes with a certain unfathomable candor, of which she had the secret.

"Here," she said, "is a letter which I think you ought to see at once, Professor Elmore"; and she gave him the note with an air of unconcern, which he afterward recalled without being able to determine whether it was real indifference or only the calm resulting from the transfer of the whole responsibility to him. She stood looking at him while he read:

MISS,

In this evening I am just arrived from Venise, 4 hours afterwards I have had the fortune to see you and to speake with you — and to favorite me of your gentil acquaintance-ship at rail-away. I never forgeet the moments I have seen you. Your pretty and nice figure had attached my heard so much, that I deserted in the hopiness to see you at Venise. And I was so lukely to speak with you cut too short, and in the possibility to understand all. I wished to go also in this Sonday to Venise, but I am sory that I cannot, beaucause I must feeled now the consequences of the desertation. Pray Miss to agree the assurance of my lov, and perhaps I will be so lukely to receive a notice from you Miss if I can hop a little (hapiness) sympathie. Très humble

E. VON EHRHARDT.

Elmore was not destitute of the national sense of humor; but he read this letter not only without amusement in its English, but with intense bitter-

ness and renewed alarm. It appeared to him that
the willingness of the ladies to put the affair in his
hands had not strongly manifested itself till it had
quite passed their own control, and had become a
most embarrassing difficulty,—when, in fact, it was
no longer a merit in them to confide it to him. In
the resentment of that moment, his suspicions even
accused his wife of desiring, from idle curiosity and
sentiment, the accidental meeting which had resulted
in this fresh aggression.

"Why did you show me this letter?" he asked
harshly.

"Mrs. Elmore told me to do so," Lily answered.

"Did *you* wish me to see it?"

"I don't suppose I *wished* you to see it: I
thought you ought to see it."

Elmore felt himself relenting a little. "What do
you want done about it?" he asked more gently.

"That is what I wished you to tell me," replied
the girl.

"I can't tell you what you wish me to do, but I
can tell you this, Miss Mayhew: this man's behavior
is totally irregular. He would not think of writing
to an Italian or German girl in this way. If he
desired to — to — pay attention to her, he would
write to her father."

"Yes, that's what Mrs. Elmore said. She said she supposed he must think it was the American way."

"Mrs. Elmore," began her husband; but he arrested himself there, and said, "Very well. I want to know what I am to do. I want your full and explicit authority before I act. We will dismiss the fact of irregularity. We will suppose that it is fit and becoming for a gentleman who has twice met a young lady by accident — or once by accident, and once by his own insistence — to write to her. Do you wish to continue the correspondence ? "

"No."

Elmore looked into the eyes which dwelt full upon him, and, though they were clear as the windows of heaven, he hesitated. "I must do what you *say*, no matter what you mean, you know ? "

"I mean what I say."

"Perhaps," he suggested, "you would prefer to return him this letter with a few lines on your card."

"No. I should like him to know that I have shown it to you. I should think it a liberty for an American to write to me in that way after such a short acquaintance, and I don't see why I should tolerate it from a foreigner, though I suppose their customs *are* different."

"Then you wish me to write to him ? "

"Yes."

"And make an end of the matter, once for all ?"

"Yes —."

"Very well, then."   Elmore sat down at once, and wrote : —

SIR, — Miss Mayhew has handed me your note of yester-day, and begs me to express her very great surprise that you should have ventured to address her.   She desires me also to add that you will consider at an end whatever acquain-tance you suppose yourself to have formed with her.

Your obedient servant,

OWEN ELMORE.

He handed the note to Lily.   "Yes, that will do," she said, in a low, steady voice.   She drew a deep breath, and, laying the letter softly down, went out of the room into Mrs. Elmore's.

Elmore had not had time to kindle his sealing-wax when his wife appeared swiftly upon the scene.

"I want to see what you have written, Owen," she said.

"Don't talk to me, Celia," he replied, thrusting the wax into the candle-light.   "You have put this affair entirely in my hands, and Lily approves of what I have written.   I am sick of the thing, and I don't want any more talk about it."

"I *must* see it," said Mrs. Elmore, with finality, and possessed herself of the note.   She ran it through, and then flung it on the table and dropped into a chair, while the tears started to her eyes. "What a cold, cutting, merciless letter !" she cried.

"I hope he will think so," said Elmore, gathering it up from the table, and sealing it securely in its envelope.

"You're not going to *send* it !" exclaimed his wife.

"Yes, I am."

"I did n't suppose you could be so heartless."

"Very well, then, I *won't* send it," said Elmore. "I put the affair in *your* hands. What are you going to do about it ? "

"Nonsense !"

"On the contrary, I'm perfectly serious. I don't see why you should n't manage the business. The gentleman is an acquaintance of yours. *I* don't know him." Elmore rose and put his hands in his pockets. "What do you intend to do ? Do you like this clandestine sort of thing to go on ? I dare say the fellow only wishes to amuse himself by a flirtation with a pretty American. But the question is whether you wish him to do so. I'm willing to lay his conduct to a misunderstanding of our customs, and to suppose that he thinks this is the way Americans do. I take the matter at its best: he speaks to Lily on the train without an introduction ; he joins you in your walk without invitation; he writes to her without leave, and proposes to get up a correspondence. It is all perfectly right and proper, and will appear so to Lily's friends when they hear of it. But I'm curious to know how you're going to manage the sequel. Do you wish the affair to go on, and how long do you wish it to go on?"

"You know very well that I don't wish it to go on."

"Then you wish it broken off?"

"Of course I do."

"How?"

"I think there is such a thing as acting kindly and considerately. I don't see anything in Captain Ehrhardt's conduct that calls for *savage* treatment," said Mrs. Elmore.

"You would like to have him stopped, but stopped gradually. Well, I don't wish to be savage, either, and I will act upon any suggestion of yours. I want Lily's people to feel that we managed not only wisely but humanely in checking a man who was resolved to force his acquaintance upon her."

Mrs. Elmore thought a long while. Then she said: "Why, of course, Owen, you're right about it. There *is* no other way. There could n't be any kindness in checking him gradually. But I wish," she added sor-

rowfully, " that he had not been such a *complete* goose ;
and then we could have done something with him."

"I am obliged to him for the perfection which
you regret, my dear.   If he had been less complete,
he would have been much harder to manage."

"Well," said Mrs. Elmore, rising, "I shall always
say that he meant well.   But send the letter."

Her husband did not wait for a second bidding.
He carried it himself to the general post-office that
there might be no mistake and no delay about it;
and a man who believed that he had a feeling and
tender heart experienced a barbarous joy in the inflic-
tion of this pitiless snub.   I do not say that it would
not have been different if he had trusted at all in
the sincerity of Captain Ehrhardt's passion; but he
was glad to discredit it.   A misgiving to the other
effect would have complicated the matter.   But now
he was perfectly free to disembarrass himself of a
trouble which had so seriously threatened his peace.
He was responsible to Miss Mayhew's family, and Mrs.
Elmore herself could not say, then or afterward, that
there was any other way open to him.   I will not
contend that his motives were wholly unselfish.   No
doubt a sense of personal annoyance, of offended decorum, of wounded respectability, qualified the zeal
for Miss Mayhew's good which prompted him.   He

was still a young and inexperienced man, confronted
with a strange perplexity: he did the best he could,
and I suppose it was the best that could be done.
At any rate, he had no regrets, and he went cheerfully
about the work of interesting Miss Mayhew in the
monuments and memories of the city.

Since the decisive blow had been struck, the ladies
seemed to share his relief. The pursuit of Captain
Ehrhardt, while it flattered, might well have alarmed,
and the loss of a not unpleasant excitement was made
good by a sense of perfect security. Whatever repin-
ing Miss Mayhew indulged was secret, or confided
solely to Mrs. Elmore. To Elmore himself she appeared in better spirits than at first, or at least in a
more equable frame of mind. To be sure, he did not
notice very particularly. He took her to the places
and told her the things that she ought to be interested
in, and he conceived a better opinion of her mind from
the quick intelligence with which she entered into
his own feelings in regard to them, though he never
could see any evidence of the over-study for which
she had been taken from school. He made her, like
Mrs. Elmore, the partner of his historical researches;
he read his notes to both of them now; and when his
wife was prevented from accompanying him, he went
with Lily alone to visit the scenes of such events as

his researches concerned, and to fill his mind with the local color which he believed would give life and character to his studies of the past. They also went often to the theatre; and, though Lily could not understand the plays, she professed to be entertained, and she had a grateful appreciation of all his efforts in her behalf that amply repaid him. He grew fond of her society; he took a childish pleasure in having people in the streets turn and glance at the handsome girl by his side, of whose beauty and stylishness he became aware through the admiration looked over the shoulders of the Austrians, and openly spoken by the Italian populace. It did not occur to him that she might not enjoy the growth of their acquaintance in equal degree, that she fatigued herself with the appreciation of the memorable and the beautiful, and that she found these long rambles rather dull. He was a man of little conversation; and, unless Mrs. Elmore was of the company, Miss Mayhew pursued his pleasures for the most part in silence. One evening, at the end of the week, his wife asked, "Why do you always take Lily through the Piazza on the side farthest from where the officers sit? Are you afraid of her meeting Captain Ehrhardt?"

"Oh, no! I consider the Ehrhardt business settled.

But you know the Italians never walk on the officers' side."

"You are not an Italian. What do you gain by flattering them up? I should think you might suppose a young girl had some curiosity."

"I do; and I do everything I can to gratify her curiosity. I went to San Pietro di Castello to-day, to show her where the Brides of Venice were stolen."

"The oldest and dirtiest part of the city! What *could* the child care for the Brides of Venice? Now be reasonable, Owen!"

"It 's a romantic story. I thought girls liked such things, — about getting married."

"And that 's the reason you took her yesterday to show her the Bucentaur that the doges wedded the Adriatic in! Well, what was your idea in going with her to the Cemetery of San Michele?"

"I thought she would be interested. I had never been there before myself, and I thought it would be a good opportunity to verify a passage I was at work on. We always show people the cemetery at home."

"That was considerate. And why did you go to Canarregio on Wednesday?"

"I wished her to see the statue of Sior Antonio Rioba; you know it was the Venetian Pasquino in the Revolution of '48 — "

"Charming!"

"And the Campo di Giustizia, where the executions used to take place."

"Delightful!"

"And — and — the house of Tintoretto," faltered Elmore.

"Delicious! She cares so much for Tintoretto! And you've been with her to the Jewish burying-ground at the Lido, and the Spanish synagogue in the Ghetto, and the fish-market at the Rialto, and you've shown her the house of Othello and the house of Desdemona, and the prisons in the ducal palace; and three nights you've taken us to the Piazza as soon as the Austrian band stopped playing, and all the interesting promenading was over, and those stuffy old Italians began to come to the caffès. Well, I can tell you that's no way to amuse a young girl. We must do something for her, or she will die. She has come here from a country where girls have always had the best time in the world, and where the times are livelier now than they ever were, with all this excitement of the war going on; and here she is dropped down in the midst of this absolute deadness: no calls, no picnics, no parties, no dances — nothing! We must do something for her."

"Shall we give her a ball?" asked Elmore, looking round the pretty little apartment.

"There's nothing going on among the Italians. But you might get us invited to the German Casino."

"I dare say. But I will not do that."

"Then we could go to the Luogotenenza, to the receptions. Mr. Hoskins could call with us, and they would send us cards."

"That would make us simply odious to the Venetians, and our house would be thronged with officers. What I've seen of them does n't make me particularly anxious for the honor of their further acquaintance."

"Well, I don't ask you to do any of these things," said Mrs. Elmore, who had, in fact, mentioned them with the intention of insisting upon an abated claim. "But I think you *might* go and dine at one of the hotels — at the Danieli — instead of that Italian restaurant; and then Lily could see somebody at the table d'hôte, and not simply *perish* of despair."

"I — I did n't suppose it was so bad as that," said Elmore.

"Why, of course, she has n't said anything, — she's far too well-bred for that; but I can tell from my own feelings how she must suffer. I have you, Owen," she said tenderly, "but Lily has *nobody*. She has gone through this Ehrhardt business so well that I think we ought to do all we can to divert her mind."

"Well, now, Celia, you see the difficulty of our position, — the nature of the responsibility we have assumed. How are we possibly, here in Venice, to divert the mind of a young lady fresh from the parties and picnics of Patmos?"

"We can go and dine at the Danieli," replied Mrs. Elmore.

"Very well, let us go, then. But she will learn no Italian there. She will hear nothing but English from the travellers and bad French from the waiters; while at our restaurant — "

"Pshaw!" cried Mrs. Elmore, "what does Lily care for Italian? I'm sure *I* never want to hear another word of it."

At this desperate admission, Elmore quite gave way; he went to the Danieli the next morning, and arranged to begin dining there that day. There is no denying that Miss Mayhew showed an enthusiasm in prospect of the change that even the sight of the pillar to which Foscarini was hanged head downwards for treason to the Republic had not evoked. She made herself look very pretty, and she was visibly an impression at the table d' hôte when she sat down there. Elmore had found places opposite an elderly lady and quite a young gentleman, of English speech, but of not very English effect otherwise, who bowed

to Lily in acknowledgment of some former meeting.
The old lady said, "So you've reached Venice at last?
I'm very pleased, for your sake," as if at some point
of the progress thither she had been privy to anxieties of Lily about arriving at her destination; and,
in fact, they had been in the same hotels at Marseilles
and Genoa. The young gentleman said nothing, but
he looked at Lily throughout the dinner, and seemed
to take his eyes from her only when she glanced at
him; then he dropped his gaze to his neglected plate
and blushed. When they left the table, he made
haste to join the Elmores in the reading-room, where
he contrived, with creditable skill, to get Lily apart
from them for the examination of an illustrated
newspaper, at which neither of them looked; they
remained chatting and laughing over it in entire
irrelevancy till the elderly lady rose and said, "Herbert, Herbert! I am ready to go now," upon which
he did not seem at all so, but went submissively.

"Who are those people, Lily?" asked Mrs. Elmore,
as they walked towards Florian's for their after-dinner coffee. The Austrian band was playing in the
centre of the Piazza, and the tall, blond German
officers promenaded back and forth with dark Hungarian women, who looked each like a princess of
her race. The lights glittered upon them, and on

the brilliant groups spread fan-wise out into the Piazza before the caffès; the scene seemed to shake and waver in the splendor, like something painted.

"Oh, their name is Andersen, or something like that; and they 're from Helgoland, or some such place. I saw them first in Paris, but we did n't speak till we got to Marseilles. That 's his aunt; they 're English subjects, someway; and he 's got an appointment in the civil service — I think he called it — in India, and he does n't want to go; and I told him he ought to go to America. That 's what I tell all these Europeans."

"It 's the best advice for them," said Mrs. Elmore.

"They don't seem in any great haste to act upon it," laughed Miss Mayhew. "Who was the red-faced young man that seemed to know you, and stared so ?"

"That 's an English artist who is staying here. He has a curious name, — Rose-Black; and he is the most impudent and pushing man in the world. I would n't introduce him, because I saw he was just dying for it."

Miss Mayhew laughed, as she laughed at everything, not because she was amused, but because she was happy; this childlike gayety of heart was great part of her charm.

Elmore had quieted his scruples as a good Venetian by coming inside of the caffè while the band played, instead of sitting outside with the bad patriots; but he put the ladies next the window, and so they were not altogether sacrificed to his sympathy with the *dimostrazione*.

VII.

THE next morning Elmore was called from his bed — at no very early hour, it must be owned, but at least before a nine o'clock breakfast — to see a gentleman who was waiting in the parlor. He dressed hurriedly, with a thousand exciting speculations in his mind, and found Mr. Rose-Black looking from the balcony window. "You have a pleasant position here," he said easily, as he turned about to meet Elmore's look of indignant demand. "I've come to ask all about our friends the Andersens."

"I don't know anything about them," answered Elmore. "I never saw them before."

"Áöh!" said the painter. Elmore had not invited him to sit down, but now he dropped into a chair, with the air of asking Elmore to explain himself. "The young lady of your party seemed to know them. How uncommonly pretty all your American young girls are! But I'm told they fade very soon. I should like to make up a picnic party with you all for the Lido."

"Thank you," replied Elmore stiffly. "Miss Mayhew has seen the Lido."

"Aöh! *That's* her name. It's a pretty name."
He looked through the open door into the dining-
room, where the table was set for breakfast, with the
usual water-goblet at each plate. "I see you have
beer for breakfast. There's nothing so nice, you
know. Would you — would you mind giving me a
glahs?"

Through an undefined sense of the duties of hos-
pitality, Elmore was surprised by this impudence into
sending out to the next caffè for a pitcher of beer.
Rose-Black poured himself out one glass and another
till he had emptied the pitcher, conversing affably
meanwhile with his silent host.

"*Why* didn't you turn him out of doors?" demanded Mrs. Elmore, as soon as the painter's departure allowed her to slip from the closed door behind
which she had been imprisoned in her room.

"I did everything *but* that," replied her husband,
whom this interview had saddened more than it had
angered.

"You sent out for beer for him!"

"I didn't know but it might make him sick.
Really, the thing is incredible. I think the man is
cracked."

"He is an Englishman, and he thinks he can take any kind of liberty with us because we are Americans."

"That seems to be the prevalent impression among all the European nationalities," said Elmore. "Let's drop him for the present, and try to be more brutal in the future."

Mrs. Elmore, so far from dropping him, turned to Lily, who entered at that moment, and recounted the extraordinary adventure of the morning, which scarcely needed the embellishment of her fancy; it was not really a gallon of beer, but a quart, that Mr. Rose-Black had drunk. She enlarged upon previous aggressions of his, and said finally that they had to thank Mr. Ferris for his acquaintance.

"Ferris could n't help himself," said Elmore. "He apologized to me afterward. The man got him into a corner. But he warned us about him as soon he could. And Rose-Black would have made our acquaintance, any way. I believe he's crazy."

"I don't see how that helps the matter."

"It helps to explain it," concluded Elmore, with a sigh. "We can't refer everything to our being American lambs, and his being a ravening European wolf."

"Of course he came round to find out about Lily,"

said Mrs. Elmore. "The Andersens were a mere blind."

"Oh, Mrs. Elmore!" cried Lily in deprecation.

The bell jangled. "That is the postman," said Mrs. Elmore.

There was a home-letter for Lily, and one from Lily's sister enclosed to Mrs. Elmore. The ladies rent them open, and lost themselves in the cross-written pages; and neither of them saw the dismay with which Elmore looked at the handwriting of the envelope addressed to him. His wife vaguely knew that he had a letter, and meant to ask him for it as soon as she should have finished her own. When she glanced at him again, he was staring at the smiling face of Miss Mayhew, as she read her letter, with the wild regard of one who sees another in mortal peril, and can do nothing to avert the coming doom, but must dumbly await the catastrophe.

"What is it, Owen?" asked his wife in a low voice.

He started from his trance, and struggled to answer quietly. "I 've a letter here which I suppose I 'd better show to you first."

They rose and went into the next room, Miss Mayhew following them with a bright, absent look, and then dropping her eyes again to her letter.

Elmore put the note he had received into his wife's hands without a word.

SIR, — My position permitted me to take a woman. I am a soldier, but I am an engineer — operateous, and I can exercise wherever my profession in the civil life. I have seen Miss Mayhew, and I have great sympathie for she. I think I will be lukely with her, if Miss Mayhew would be of the same intention of me.

If you believe, Sir, that my open and realy proposition will not offendere Miss Mayhew, pray to handed to her this note. Pray sir to excuse me the liberty to fatigue you, and to go over with silence if you would be of another intention.

Your obedient servant,

E. VON EHRHARDT.

Mrs. Elmore folded the letter carefully up and returned it to her husband. If he had perhaps dreaded some triumphant outburst from her, he ought to have been content with the thoroughly daunted look which she lifted to his, and the silence in which she suffered him to do justice to the writer.

"This is the letter of a gentleman, Celia," he said.

"Yes," she responded faintly.

"It puts another complexion on the affair entirely."

"Yes. Why did he wait a whole week?" she added.

"It is a serious matter with him. He had a right

to take time for thinking it over." Elmore looked at the date of the Peschiera postmark, and then at that of Venice on the back of the envelope. " No, he wrote at once. This has been kept in the Venetian office, and probably read there by the authorities."

His wife did not heed the conjecture. " He began all wrong," she grieved. " Why could n't he have behaved sensibly ? "

" We must look at it from another point of view now," replied Elmore. " He has repaired his error by this letter."

" No, no ; he has n't."

" The question is now what to do about the changed situation. This is an offer of marriage. It comes in the proper way. It 's a very sincere and manly letter. The man has counted the whole cost : he 's ready to leave the army and go to America, if she says so. He 's in love. How can she refuse him ? "

" Perhaps she is n't in love with him," said Mrs. Elmore.

" Oh ! That 's true. I had n't thought of that. Then it 's very simple."

" But I don't know that she is n't," murmured Mrs. Elmore.

" Well, ask her."

" How could *she* tell ? "

" How could she *tell ?* "

" Yes.   Do you suppose a child like that can know her own mind in an instant ? "

" I should think she could."

" Well, she could n't.   She liked the excitement, — the romanticality of it; but she does n't know any more than you or I whether she cares for him.   I don't suppose marriage with anybody has ever seriously entered her head yet."

" It will have to do so now," said Elmore firmly. " There's no help for it."

" I think the American plan is much better," pouted Mrs. Elmore.   " It 's horrid to know that a man 's in love with you, and wants to marry you, from the very start.   Of course it makes you hate him."

" I dare say the American plan is better in this as in most other things.   But we can't discuss abstractions, Celia.   We must come down to business.   What are we to do ? "

" I don't know."

" We must submit the question to her."

" To that innocent, unsuspecting little thing? Never ! " cried Mrs. Elmore.

" Then we must decide it, as he seems to expect we may, without reference to her," said her husband.

" No, that won't do. Let me think." Mrs. Elmore thought to so little purpose that she left the word to her husband again.

" You see we must lay the matter before her."

" Could n't — could n't we let him come to see us awhile ? Could n't we explain our ways to him, and allow him to pay her attentions without letting her know about this letter ? "

" I 'm afraid he would n't understand, — that we could n't make it clear to him," said Elmore. " If we invited him to the house he would consider it as an acceptance. He wants a categorical answer, and he has a right to it. It would be no kindness to a man with his ideas to take him on probation. He has behaved honorably, and we 're bound to consider him."

" Oh, I don't think he 's done anything so very great," said Mrs. Elmore, with that disposition we all have to disparage those who put us in difficulties.

" He 's done everything he could do," said Elmore. " Shall I speak to Miss Mayhew ? "

" No, you had better let me," sighed his wife. " I suppose we must. But I think it 's horrid ! Everything could have gone on so nicely if he had n't been so impatient from the beginning. Of course she won't have him now. She will be scared, and that will be the end of it." ·

"I think you ought to be just to him, Celia. I can't help feeling for him. He has thrown himself upon our mercy, and he has a claim to right and thoughtful treatment."

"She won't have anything to do with him. You'll see."

"I shall be very glad of that," Elmore began.

"*Why* should you be glad of it?" demanded his wife.

He laughed. "I think I can safely leave his case in your hands. Don't go to the other extreme. If she married a German, he would let her black his boots, — like that general in Munich."

"Who is talking of marriage?" retorted Mrs. Elmore.

"Captain Ehrhardt and I. That's what it comes to; and it can't come to anything else. I like his courage in writing English, and it's wonderful how he hammers his meaning into it. 'Lukely' isn't bad, is it? And 'my position permitted me to take a woman' — I suppose he means that he has money enough to marry on — is delicious. Upon my word, I have a good deal of sympathie for he!"

"For shame, Owen! It's wicked to make fun of his English."

"My dear, I respect him for writing in English.

The whole letter is touchingly brave and fine. Confound him! I wish I had never heard of him. What does he come bothering across my path for?"

"Oh, don't feel that way about it, Owen!" cried his wife. "It's cruel."

"I don't. I wish to treat him in the most generous manner; after all, it is n't his fault. But you must allow, Celia, that it's very annoying and extremely perplexing. *We* can't make up Miss Mayhew's mind for her. Even if we found out that she liked him, it would be only the beginning of our troubles. *We've* no right to give her away in marriage, or let her involve her affections here. But be judicious, Celia."

"It's easy enough to say that!"

"I'll be back in an hour," said Elmore. "I'm going to the Square. We must n't lose time."

As he passed out through the breakfast-room, Lily was sitting by the window with her letter in her lap, and a happy smile on her lips. When he came back she happened to be seated in the same place; she still had a letter in her lap, but she was smiling no longer; her face was turned from him as he entered, and he imagined a wistful droop in that corner of her mouth which showed on her profile.

But she rose very promptly, and with a heightened color said, "I am sorry to trouble you to answer another letter for me, Professor Elmore. I manage my correspondence at home myself, but here it seems to be different."

"It need n't be different here, Lily," said Elmore kindly. "You can answer all the letters you receive in just the way you like. We don't doubt your discretion in the least. We will abide by any decision of yours, on any point that concerns yourself."

"Thank you," replied the girl; "but in this case I think you had better write." She kept slipping Ehrhardt's letter up and down between her thumb and finger against the palm of her left hand, and delayed giving it to him, as if she wished him to say something first.

"I suppose you and Celia have talked the matter over?"

"Yes."

"And I hope you have determined upon the course you are going to take, quite uninfluenced?"

"Oh, quite so."

"I feel bound to tell you," said Elmore, "that this gentleman has now done everything that we could expect of him, and has fully atoned for any error he committed in making your acquaintance."

"Yes, I understand that. Mrs. Elmore thought

he might have written because he saw he had gone too far, and could n't think of any other way out of it."

"That occurred to me, too, though I did n't mention it. But we 're bound to take the letter on its face, and that 's open and honorable. Have you made up your mind ?"

"Yes."

"Do you wish for delay ? There is no reason for haste."

"There 's no reason for delay, either," said the girl. Yet she did not give up the letter, or show any signs of intending to terminate the interview. "If I had had more experience, I should know how to act better; but I must do the best I can, without the experience. I think that even in a case like this we should try to do right, don't you ?"

"Yes, above all other cases," said Elmore, with a laugh.

She flushed in recognition of her absurdity. "I mean that we ought n't to let our feelings carry us away. I saw so many girls carried away by their feelings, when the first regiments went off, that I got a horror of it. I think it 's wicked: it deceives both ; and then you don't know how to break the engagement afterward."

"You're quite right, Lily," said Elmore, with a rising respect for the girl.

"Professor Elmore, can you believe that, with all the attentions I've had, I've never seriously thought of getting married as the end of it all?" she asked, looking him freely in the eyes.

"I can't understand it, — no man could, I suppose, — but I do believe it. Mrs. Elmore has often told me the same thing."

"And this — letter — it — means marriage."

"That and nothing else. The man who wrote it would consider himself cruelly wronged if you accepted his attentions without the distinct purpose of marrying him."

She drew a deep breath. "I shall have to ask you to write a refusal for me." But still she did not give him the letter.

"Have you made up your mind to that?"

"I can't make up my mind to anything else."

Elmore walked unhappily back and forth across the room. "I have seen something of international marriages since I've been in Europe," he said. "Sometimes they succeed; but generally they're wretched failures. The barriers of different race, language, education, religion, — they're terrible barriers. It's very hard for a man and woman to understand each other at the best; with these differences added, it's almost a hopeless case."

"Yes; that's what Mrs. Elmore said."

"And suppose you were married to an Austrian officer stationed in Italy. You would have *no* society outside of the garrison. Every other human creature that looked at you would hate you. And if you were ordered to some of those half barbaric principalities, — Moldavia or Wallachia, or into Hungary or Bohemia, — everywhere your husband would be an instrument for the suppression of an alien or disaffected population. What a fate for an American girl!"

"If he were good," said the girl, replying in the abstract, "she need n't care."

"If he were good, you need n't care. No. And he might leave the Austrian service, and go with you to America, as he hints. What could he do there? He might get an appointment in our army, though that's not so easy now; or he might go to Patmos, and live upon your friends till he found something to do in civil life."

Lily began a laugh. "Why, Professor Elmore, *I* don't want to marry him! What in the world are you arguing with me for?"

"Perhaps to convince myself. I feel that I ought n't to let these considerations weigh as a feather in the

balance if you are at all—at all—ahem! excuse me!
—attached to him. That, of course, outweighs everything else."

"But I 'm *not!*" cried the girl. "How *could* I be?
I 've only met him twice. It would be perfectly
ridiculous. I *know* I 'm not. I ought to know that
if I know anything."

Years afterward it occurred to Elmore, when he
awoke one night, and his mind without any reason
flew back to this period in Venice, that she might
have been referring the point to him for decision.
But now it only seemed to him that she was adding
force to her denial ; and he observed nothing hysterical in the little laugh she gave.

"Well, then, we can't have it over too soon. I 'll
write now, if you will give me his letter."

She put it behind her. "Professor Elmore," she
said, "I am not going to have you think that he
ever behaved in the least presumingly. And whatever you think of me, I must tell you that I suppose
I talked very freely with him, — just as freely, as I
should with an American. I did n't know any better.
He was very interesting, and I was homesick, and so
glad to see any one who could speak English. I
suppose I was a goose; but I felt very far away
from all my friends, and I was grateful for his

kindness. Even if he had never written this last letter, I should always have said that he was a true gentleman."

"Well?"

"That is all. I can't have him treated as if he were an adventurer."

"You want him dismissed?"

"Yes."

"A man can't distinguish as to the terms of a dismissal. They're always insolent,—more insolent than ever if you try to make them kindly. I should merely make this as short and sharp as possible.'"

"Yes," she said breathlessly, as if the idea affected her respiration.

"But I will show it to you, and I won't send it without your approval."

"Thank you. But I shall not want to see it. I'd rather not." She was going out of the room.

"Will you leave me his letter? You can have it again."

She turned red in giving it him. "I forgot. Why, it's written to you, anyway!" she cried, with a laugh, and put the letter on the table.

The two doors opened and closed: one excluded Lily, and the other admitted Mrs. Elmore.

"Owen, I approve of all you said, except that

about the form of the refusal. *I* will read what you say. I intend that it *shall* be made kindly."

" Very well. I 'll copy a letter of yours, or write from your dictation."

" No ; you write it, and I 'll criticise it."

" Oh, you talk as if I were eager to write the letter ! Can't you imagine it 's being a very painful thing to me ? " he demanded.

" It did n't seem to be so before."

" Why, the situation was n't the same before he wrote this letter ! "

" I don't see how. He was as much in earnest then as he is now, and you had no pity for him."

" Oh, my goodness ! " cried Elmore desperately. " Don't you see the difference ? He had n't given any proof before " —

" Oh, proof, proof ! You men are always wanting proof ! What better proof could he have given than the way he followed her about ? Proof, indeed ! I suppose you 'd like to have Lily prove that she does n't care for him ! "

" Yes," said Elmore sadly, " I should like very much to have her prove it."

" Well, you won't get her to. What makes you think she does ? "

" I don't. Do you ? "

" N-o," answered Mrs. Elmore reluctantly.

" Celia, Celia, you will drive me mad if you go
on in this way! The girl has told me, over and over,
that she wishes him dismissed. Why do you think
she does n't ? "

" I don't. Who hinted such a thing ? But I don't
want you to *enjoy* doing it."

" *Enjoy* it ? So you think I enjoy it! What do
you suppose I'm made of ? Perhaps you think I
enjoyed catechizing the child about her feelings
toward him ? Perhaps you think I enjoy the whole
confounded affair ? Well, I give it up. I will let
it go. If I can't have your full and hearty support,
I 'll let it go. I 'll do nothing about it."

He threw Ehrhardt's letter on the table, and went
and sat down by the window. His wife took the
letter up and read it over. " Why, you see he asks
you to pass it over in silence if you don't consent."

" Does he ?" asked Elmore. " I had n't noticed that."

" Perhaps you 'd better read some of your letters,
Owen, before you answer them ! "

" Really, I had forgotten. I had forgotten that the
letter was written to me at all. I thought it was to
Lily, and she had got to thinking so too. Well, then,
I won't do anything about it." He drew a breath of
relief.

"Perhaps," suggested his wife, " he asked that so as to leave himself some hope if he should happen to meet her again."

" And we don't wish him to have any hope."

Mrs. Elmore was silent.

"Celia," cried her husband indignantly, "I can't have you playing fast and loose with me in this matter!"

"I suppose I may have time to think?" she retorted.

"Yes, if you will tell me what you *do* think; but that I *must* know. It's a thing too vital in its consequences for me to act without your full concurrence. I won't take another step in it till I know just how far you have gone with me. If I may judge of what this man's influence upon Lily would be by the fact that he has brought us to the verge of the only real quarrel we've ever had" —

"Who's quarrelling, Owen?" asked Mrs. Elmore meekly. " I 'm not."

" Well, well! we won't dispute about that. I want to know whether you thought with me that it was improper for him to address her in the car?"

"Yes."

"And still more improper for him to join you in the street?"

"Yes. But he was very gentlemanly."

"No matter about that. You were just as much annoyed as I was by his letter to her?"

"I don't know about annoyed. It scared me."

"Very well. And you approved of my answering it as I did?"

"I had nothing to do with it. I thought you were acting conscientiously. I'll say that much."

"You've got to say more. You have got to say you approved of it; for you know you did."

"Oh — *approved* of it? Yes!"

"That's all I want. Now I agree with you that if we pass this letter in silence, it will leave him with some hope. You agree with me that in a marriage between an American girl and an Austrian officer the chances would be ninety-nine to a hundred against her happiness at the best."

"There are a great many unhappy marriages at home," said Mrs. Elmore impartially.

"That is n't the point, Celia, and you know it. The point is whether you believe the chances are for or against her in such a marriage. Do you?"

"Do I what?"

"Agree with me?"

"Yes; but I say they *might* be *very* happy. I shall always say that."

Elmore flung up his hands in despair. "Well, then, say what shall be done now."

This was perhaps just what Mrs. Elmore did not choose to say. She was silent a long time, — so long that Elmore said, "But there's really no haste about it," and took some notes of his history out of a drawer, and began to look them over, with his back turned to her.

"I never knew anything so heartless!" she cried. "Owen, this *must* be attended to at once! I can't have it hanging over me any longer. It will make me sick."

He turned abruptly round, and, seating himself at the table, wrote a note, which he pushed across to her. It acknowledged the receipt of Captain von Ehrhardt's letter, and expressed Miss Mayhew's feeling that there was nothing in it to change her wish that the acquaintance should cease. In after years, the terms of this note did not always appear to Elmore wisely chosen or humanely considered; but he stood at bay, and he struck mercilessly. In spite of the explicit concurrence of both Miss Mayhew and his wife, he felt as if they were throwing wholly upon him a responsibility whose fearfulness he did not then realize. Even in his wife's "Send it!" he was aware of a subtile reservation on her part.

VIII.

MRS. ELMORE and Lily again rose buoyantly from the conclusive event, but he succumbed to it. For the delicate and fastidious invalid, keeping his health evenly from day to day upon the condition of a free and peaceful mind, the strain had been too much. He had a bad night, and the next day a gastric trouble declared itself which kept him in bed half the week, and left him very weak and tremulous. His friends did not forget him during this time. Hoskins came regularly to see him, and supplied his place at the table d'hôte of the Danieli, going to and fro with the ladies, and efficiently protecting them from the depredations of the Austrian soldiery. From Mr. Rose-Black he could not protect them; and both the ladies amused Elmore with a dramatization of how the Englishman had boldly outwitted them, and trampled all their finessing under foot, by simply walking up to them in the reading-room, and saying, "This is Miss Mayhew, I suppose," and putting himself at once on the footing of an old family friend. They read to Elmore, and they put his papers in order, so that he did not know where to find anything when he got well; but they always came home from the hotel with some lively gossip, and this he liked. They professed to recognize an anxiety on the part of Mr. Andersen's aunt that his mind should not be diverted from the civil service in India by thoughts of young American ladies; but she sent some delicacies to Elmore, and one day she even came to call with her nephew, in extreme reluctance and anxiety as they pretended to him.

The next afternoon the young man called alone, and Elmore, who was now on foot, received him in the parlor, before the ladies came in. Mr. Andersen had a bunch of flowers in one hand, and a small wooden box containing a little turtle on a salad-leaf in the other; the poor animals are sold in the Piazza at Venice for souvenirs of the city, and people often carry them away. Elmore took the offerings simply, as he took everything in life, and interpreted them as an expression, however odd, of Mr. Andersen's sympathy with his recent sufferings, of which he gave him some account; but he practised a decent self-denial, here, and they were already talking of the weather when the ladies appeared. He hastened to exhibit the tokens of Mr. Andersen's kind remembrance, and was mystified by the young man's confusion, and the impatient, almost contemptuous, air with which his wife listened to him. Hoskins came in at that moment to ask about Elmore's health, and showed the hostile civility to Andersen which young men use toward each other in the presence of ladies; and then, seeing that the latter had secured the place at Miss Mayhew's side on the sofa, he limped to the easy chair near Mrs. Elmore, and fell into talk with her about Rose-Black's pictures, which he had just seen. They were based upon an endeavor to trace the moral principles believed by Mr. Ruskin to underlie Venetian art, and they were very queer, so Hoskins said; he roughly sketched an idea of some of them on a block he took from his pocket.

Mr. Andersen and Lily went out upon one of the high-railed balconies that overhung the canal, and stood there, with their backs to the others. She seemed to be listening, with averted face, while he, with his cheek leaning upon one hand and his elbow resting on the balcony rail, kept a pensive attitude after they had apparently ceased to speak. Something in their pose struck the sculptor's fancy, and he made a hasty sketch of them, and was showing

it to the Elmores when Lily suddenly descended into the room again, and, saying something about its being quite dark, went out, and left Mr. Andersen to make his adieux to the others. He startled them by saying that he was to set off for India in the morning, and he went away very melancholy.

"Well, I don't know," said Hoskins, thoughtfully retouching his sketch, "that I should feel very lively about going out to India myself."

"He seems to be a very affectionate young fellow," observed Elmore, "and I've no doubt he will feel the separation from his friends. But I really don't know why he should have brought me a bouquet, and a small turtle in a box, on the eve of his departure."

"What?" cried Hoskins, with a rude guffaw; and when Elmore had showed his gifts, Hoskins threw back his head and laughed indecently. His behavior nettled Elmore, and it sent Mrs. Elmore prematurely out of the room; for, not content with his explosions of laughter, he continued for some time to amuse himself by touching up with the point of his pencil the tail of the turtle which he had turned out of its box upon the table. At Mrs. Elmore's withdrawal he stopped, and presently said good-night rather soberly.

Then she returned. "Owen," she asked sadly,

"did you really think these flowers and that turtle were for you?"

"Why, yes," he answered.

"Well, I don't know whether I would n't almost rather it had been a joke. I believe that I would rather despise your heart than your head. Why should Mr. Andersen bring *you* flowers and a turtle?"

"Upon my word, I don't know."

"They were for Lily! And your mistake has added another pang to the poor young fellow's suffering. She has just refused him," she said; and as Elmore continued to glare blankly at her, she added: "She was refusing him there on the balcony while that disgusting Mr. Hoskins was sketching them; and he had his hand up, that way, because he was crying."

"This is horrible, Celia!" cried Elmore. The scent of the flowers lying on the table seemed to choke him; the turtle clawing about on the smooth surface looked demoniacal. "Why ——"

"Now, don't ask me why she refused him, Owen. Of course she could n't care for a boy like that. But he can't realize it, and it's just as miserable for him as if he were a thousand years old."

Elmore hung his head. "It was all a mistake. But how should I know any better? I am a straight-

forward man, Celia; and I am unfit for the care
that has been thrown upon me. It's more than I
can bear. No, I'm *not* fit for it!" he cried at last;
and his wife, seeing him so crushed, now said something to console him.

"I know you're not. I see it more and more.
But I know that you will do the best you can, and
that you will always act from a good motive. Only
do try to be more on your guard."

"I will — I will," he answered humbly.

He had a temptation, the next time he visited
Hoskins, to tell him the awful secret, and to see how
the situation of that night, with this lurid light upon
it, affected him: it could do poor Andersen, now on
his way to India, no harm. He yielded to his temptation, at the same time that he confessed his own
blunder about the flowers.

Hoskins whistled. "I tell you what," he said, after
a long pause, "there are some things in history that
I never could realize, — like Mary, Queen of Scots,
for instance, putting on her best things, and stepping
down into the front parlor of that castle to have her
head off. But a thing like this, happening on your
own balcony, *helps* you to realize it."

"It helps you to realize it," assented Elmore, deeply
oppressed by the tragic parallel.

"He's just beginning to feel it about now," said Hoskins, with strange *sang froid*. "I reckon it's a good deal like being shot. I did n't fully appreciate my little hit under a couple of days. Then I began to find out that something had happened. Look here," he added, "I want to show you something;" and he pulled the wet cloth off a breadth of clay which he had set up on a board stayed against the wall. It was a bas-relief representing a female figure advancing from the left corner over a stretch of prairie towards a bulk of forest on the right; bison, bear, and antelope fled before her; a lifted hand shielded her eyes; a star lit the fillet that bound her hair.

"That's the best thing you've done, Hoskins," said Elmore. "What do you call it?"

"Well, I have n't settled yet. I *have* thought of 'Westward the Star of Empire,' but that's rather long; and I 've thought of 'American Enterprise.' I ain't in any hurry to name it. You like it, do you?"

"I like it immensely!" cried Elmore. "You must let me bring the ladies to see it."

"Well, not just yet," said the sculptor, in some confusion. "I want to get it a little further along first."

They stood looking together at the figure; and

when Elmore went away he puzzled himself about something in it, — he could not tell exactly what. He thought he had seen that face and figure before, but this is what often occurs to the connoisseur of modern sculpture. His mind heavily reverted to Lily and her suitors. Take her in one way, especially in her subordination to himself, the girl was as simply a child as any in the world, — good-hearted, tender, and sweet, and, as he could see, without tendency to flirtation. Take her in another way, confront her with a young and marriageable man, and Elmore greatly feared that she unconsciously set all her beauty and grace at work to charm him; another life seemed to inform her, and irradiate from her, apart from which she existed simple and childlike still. In the security of his own deposited affections, it appeared to him cruelly absurd that a passion which any other pretty girl might, and some other pretty girl in time must, have kindled, should cling, when once awakened, so inalienably to the pretty girl who had, in a million chances, chanced to awaken it. He wondered how much of this constancy was natural, and how much merely attributive and traditional, and whether human happiness or misery were increased by it on the whole.

IX.

In the respite which followed the dismissal of Andersen, the English painter, Rose-Black, visited the Elmores as often as the servant, who had orders in his case to say that they were *impediti*, failed of her duty. They could not always escape him at the caffè, and they would have left off dining at the hotel but for the shame of feeling that he had driven them away. If he had been an Englishman repelling their advances, instead of an Englishman pursuing them, he could not have been more offensive. He affronted their national as well as personal self-esteem; he early declared himself a sympathizer with the Southrons (as the London press then called them), and he expressed the current belief of his compatriots, that we were going to the dogs.

"What do you really make of him, Owen?" asked Mrs. Elmore, after an evening that, in its improbable discomfort, had passed quite like a nightmare.

"Well, I've been thinking a good deal about him.

I have been wondering if, in his phenomenal way, he is not a final expression of the national genius,— the stupid contempt for the rights of others; the tacit denial of the rights of any people who are at English mercy; the assumption that the courtesies and decencies of life are for use exclusively towards Englishmen."

This was in that embittered old war-time : we have since learned how forbearing and generous and amiable Englishmen are; how they never take advantage of any one they believe stronger than themselves, or fail in consideration for those they imagine their superiors; how you have but to show yourself successful in order to win their respect, and even affection.

But for the present Mrs. Elmore replied to her husband's perverted ideas, "Yes, it must be so," and she supported him in the ineffectual experiment of deferential politeness, Christian charity, broad humanity, and savage rudeness upon Rose-Black. It was all one to Rose-Black.

He took an air of serious protection towards Mrs. Elmore, and often gave her advice, while he practised an easy gallantry with Lily, and ignored Elmore altogether. His intimacy was superior to the accidents of their moods, and their slights and snubs were accepted apparently as interesting expressions of a civilization about which he was insatiably curious, especially as regarded the relations of young people. There was no mistaking the fact that Rose-Black in his way had fallen under the spell which Elmore had learned to dread; but there was nothing to be done, and he helplessly waited. He saw what must come; and one evening it came, when Rose-Black, in more than usually offensive patronage, lolled back upon the sofa at Miss Mayhew's side, and said, "About flirtations, now, in America,—tell me something about flirtations. We've heard so much about your American flirtations. We only have them with married ladies, on the continent, and I don't suppose Mrs. Elmore would think of one."

"I don't know what you mean," said Lily. "I don't know anything about flirtations."

This seemed to amuse Rose-Black as an uncommonly fine piece of American humor, which was then just beginning to make its way with the English. "Oh, but come, now, you don't expect me to believe that, you know. If you won't tell me, suppose you show me what an American flirtation is like. Suppose we get up a flirtation. How should you begin?"

The girl rose with a more imposing air than

Elmore could have imagined of her stature; but almost any woman can be awful in emergencies. " I should begin by bidding you good-evening," she answered, and swept out of the room.

Elmore felt as if he had been left alone with a man mortally hurt in combat, and were likely to be arrested for the deed. He gazed with fascination upon Rose-Black, and wondered to see him stir, and at last rise, and with some incoherent words to them, get himself away. He dared not lift his gaze to the man's eyes, lest he should see there some reflection of the pain that filled his own. He would have gone after him, and tried to say something in condolence, but he was quite helpless to move; and as he sat still, gazing at the door through which Rose-Black disappeared, Mrs. Elmore said quietly : —

"Well, really, I think that ought to be the last of him. You see, she's quite able to take care of herself when she knows her ground. You can't say that she has thrown the brunt of this affair upon you, Owen."

" I am not so sure of that," sighed Elmore. " I think I suffer less when I do it than when I see it. It's horrible."

" He deserved it, every bit," returned his wife.

"Oh, I dare say," Elmore granted. " But the sight even of justice is n't pleasant, I find."

"I don't understand you, Owen. How can you care so much for this impudent wretch's little snub, and yet be so indifferent about refusing Captain Ehrhardt?"

"I'm not indifferent about it, my dear. I know that I did right, but I don't know that I could do right under the same circumstances again."

In fact there were times when Elmore found almost insupportable the absolute conclusion to which that business had come. It is hard to believe that anything has come to an end in this world. For a time, death itself leaves the ache of an unsatisfied expectation, as if somehow the interrupted life must go on, and there is no change we make or suffer which is not denied by the sensation of daily habit. If Ehrhardt had really come back from the vague limbo to which he had been so inexorably relegated, he might only have restored the original situation in all its discomfort and apprehension; yet maintaining, as he did, this perfect silence and absence, he established a hold upon Elmore's imagination which deepened because he could not discuss the matter frankly with his wife. He weakly feared to let her know what was passing in his thoughts, lest some misconception of hers should turn them into self-accusal or urge him to some attempt at the reparation towards which he wavered. He really could have done nothing that would not have made the matter worse, and he confined himself to speculating upon the character and history of the man whom he knew only by the incoherent hearsay of two excited women, and by the brief record of hope and passion left in the notes which Lily treasured somewhere among the archives of a young girl's triumphs. He had a morbid curiosity to see these letters again, but he dared not ask for them; and indeed it would have been an idle self-indulgence: he remembered them perfectly well. Seeing Lily so indifferent, it was characteristic of him, in that safety from consequences which he chiefly loved, that he should tacitly constitute himself, in some sort, the champion of her rejected suitor, whose pain he luxuriously fancied in all its different stages and degrees. His indolent pity even developed into a sort of self-righteous abhorrence of the girl's hardness. But this was wholly within himself, and could work no sort of harm. If he never ventured to hint these feelings to his wife, he was still further from confessing them to Lily; but once he approached the subject with Hoskins in a well-guarded generality relating to the different kinds of sensibility developed by the European and American civilization. A recent suicide for love which excited all Venice at that time — an Austrian officer hopelessly attached to an Italian girl had shot himself — had suggested their talk, and given fresh poignancy to the misgivings in Elmore's mind.

"Well," said Hoskins, "those Dutch are queer. They don't look at women as respectfully as we do, and they mix up so much cabbage with their romance that you don't know exactly how to take them; and yet here you find this fellow suffering just as much as a white man because the girl's folks won't let her have him.   In fact, I don't know but he suffered more than the average American citizen.   I think we have a great deal more common sense in our love-affairs.   We respect women more than any other people, and I think we show them more true politeness; we let 'em have their way more, and get their finger into the pie right along, and it's right we should: but we don't make fools of ourselves about them, as a general rule.   We know they're awfully nice, and they know we know it; and it's a perfectly understood thing all round. We've been used to each other all our lives, and they're just as sensible as we are.   They like a fellow, when they do like him, about as well as any of 'em; but they know he's a man and a brother after all, and he's got ever so much human nature in him.   Well, now, I reckon one of these Dutch chaps, the first time

he gets a chance to speak with a pretty girl, thinks
he's got hold of a goddess, and I suppose the girl
feels just so about him.   Why, it's natural they should,
—they've never had any chance to know any better,
and your feelings *are* apt to get the upper hand of
you, at such times, anyway.   I don't blame 'em.   One
of 'em goes off and shoots himself, and the other one
feels as if she was never going to get over it.   Well,
now, look at the way Miss Lily acted in that little
business of hers : one of these girls over here would
have had her head completely turned by that adventure ; but when she couldn't see her way exactly
clear, she puts the case in your hands, and then stands
by what you do, as calm as a clock."

"It was a very perplexing thing.   I did the best I
knew," said Elmore.

"Why, of course you did," cried Hoskins, "and she
sees that as well as you or I do, and she stands by
you accordingly.   I tell you, that girl's got a cool
head."

In his soul Elmore ungratefully and inconsist-
ently wished that her heart were not equally cool ;
but he only said, "Yes, she is a good and sensible
girl.   I hope the—the—other one is equally resigned."

"Oh, *he*'ll get along," answered Hoskins, with the

indifference of one man for the sufferings of another
in such matters. We are able to offer a brother very
little comfort and scarcely any sympathy in those
unhappy affairs of the heart which move women to a
pretty compassion for a disappointed sister. A man
in love is in no wise interesting to us for that reason;
and if he is unfortunate, we hope at the farthest that
he will have better luck next time. It is only here
and there that a sentimentalist like Elmore stops to
pity him; and it is not certain that even he would
have sighed over Captain Ehrhardt if he had not
been the means of his disappointment. As it was,
he came away, feeling that doubtless Ehrhardt had
"got along," and resolved at least to spend no more
unavailing regrets upon him.

The time passed very quietly now, and if it had
not been for Hoskins, the ladies must have found it
dull. He had nothing to do, except as he made himself occupation with his art, and he willingly bestowed
on them the leisure which Elmore could not find. They
went everywhere with him, and saw the city to advantage through his efforts. Doors, closed to ordinary
curiosity, opened to the magic of his card, and he
showed a pleasure in using such little privileges as
his position gave him for their amusement. He went
upon errands for them; he was like a brother, with

something more than a brother's pliability; he came half the time to breakfast with them, and was always welcome to all. He had the gift of extracting comfort from the darkest news about the war; he was a prophet of unfailing good to the Union cause, and in many hours of despondency they willingly submitted to the authority of his greater experience, and took heart again.

"I like your indomitable hopefulness, Hoskins," said Elmore, on one of those occasions when the consul was turning defeat into victory. "There's a streak of unconscious poetry in it, just as there is in your taking up the subjects you do. I imagine that, so far as the judgment of the world goes, our fortunes are at the lowest ebb just now —"

"Oh, the world is wrong!" interrupted the consul. "Those London papers are all in the pay of the rebels."

"I mean that we have no sort of sympathy in Europe; and yet here you are, embodying in your conception of 'Westward' the arrogant faith of the days when our destiny seemed universal union and universal dominion. There is something sublime to me in your treatment of such a work at such a time. I think an Italian, for instance, if his country were involved in a life and death struggle like this of ours, would have expressed something of the anxiety and apprehension of the time in it; but this conception of yours is as serenely undisturbed by the facts of the war as if secession had taken place in another planet. There is something Greek in that repose of feeling, triumphant over circumstance. It is like the calm beauty which makes you forget the anguish of the Laocoön."

"Is that so, Professor?" said Hoskins, blushing modestly, as an artist often must in these days of creative criticism. He seemed to reflect awhile before he added, "Well, I reckon you 're partly right. If we ever did go to smash, it would take us a whole generation to find it out. We have all been raised to put so much dependence on Uncle Sam, that if the old gentleman really did pass in his checks we should only think he was lying low for a new deal. I never happened to think it out before, but I 'm pretty sure it 's so."

"Your work would n't be worth half so much to me if you had 'thought it out,'" said Elmore. "It 's the unconsciousness of the faith that makes its chief value, as I said before; and there is another thing about it that interests and pleases me still more."

"What 's that?" asked the sculptor.

"The instinctive way in which you have given the

figure an entirely American quality. There was something very familiar to me in it, the first time you showed it, but I 've only just been able to formulate my impression: I see now that while the spirit of your conception is Greek, you have given it, as you ought, the purest American expression. Your 'Westward' is no Hellenic goddess: she is a vivid and self-reliant American girl."

At these words, Hoskins reddened deeply, and seemed not to know where to look. Mrs. Elmore had the effect of escaping through the door into her own room, and Miss Mayhew ran out upon the balcony. Hoskins followed each in turn with a queer glance, and sat a moment in silence. Then he said, "Well, I reckon I must be going," and went rather abruptly, without offering to take leave of the ladies.

As soon as he was gone, Lily came in from the balcony, and whipped into Mrs. Elmore's room, from which she flashed again in swift retreat to her own, and was seen no more; and then Mrs. Elmore came back, with a flushed face, to where her husband sat mystified.

"My dear," he said gravely, "I 'm afraid you 've hurt Mr. Hoskins's feelings."

"Do you think so?" she asked; and then she burst into a wild cry of laughter. "O, Owen, Owen! you will kill me yet!"

"Really," he replied with dignity, "I don't see any occasion in what I said for this extraordinary behavior."

"Of course you don't, and that's just what makes the fun of it. So you found something familiar in Mr. Hoskins's statue from the first, did you?" she asked. "And you did n't notice anything particular in it?"

"Particular, particular?" he demanded, beginning to lose his patience at this.

"Oh," she exclaimed, "could n't you see that it was Lily, all over again?"

Elmore laughed in turn. "Why, so it is; so it is! That accounts for everything that puzzled me. I don't wonder my maunderings amused you. It *was* ridiculous, to be sure! When in the world did she give him the sittings, and how did you manage to keep it from me so well?"

"Owen!" cried his wife, with terrible severity. "You don't think that Lily would *let* him put her into it?"

"Why, I supposed — I did n't know — I don't see how he could have done it unless — "

"He did it without leave or license," said Mrs. Elmore. "We saw it all along, but he never 'let on,' as he would say, about it, and we never meant to say anything, of course."

"Then," replied Elmore, delighted with the fact, "it has been a purely unconscious piece of cerebration."

"Cerebration!" exclaimed Mrs. Elmore, with more scorn than she knew how to express. "I should think as much!"

"Well, I don't know," said Elmore, with the pique of a man who does not care to be quite trampled under foot. "I don't see that the theory is so very unphilosophical."

"Oh, not at all!" mocked his wife. "It's philosophical to the last degree. Be as philosophical as you please, Owen; I shall love you still the same." She came up to him where he sat, and twisting her arm round his face, patronizingly kissed him on top of the head. Then she released him, and left him with another burst of derision.

X.

AFTER this Elmore had such an uncomfortable feeling that he hated to see Hoskins again, and he was relieved when the sculptor failed to make his usual call, the next evening. He had not been at dinner either, and he did not reappear for several days. Then he merely said that he had been spending the time at Chioggia, with a French painter who was making some studies down there, and they all took up the old routine of their friendly life without embarrassment.

At first it seemed to Elmore that Lily was a little shy of Hoskins, and he thought that she resented his using her charm in his art; but before the evening wore away, he lost this impression. They all got into a long talk about home, and she took her place at the piano and played some of the war-songs that had begun to supersede the old negro melodies. Then she wandered back to them, with fingers that idly drifted over the keys, and ended with " Stop dat knockin',"

in which Hoskins joined with his powerful bass in
the recitative "Let me in," and Elmore himself had
half a mind to attempt a part. The sculptor rose as
she struck the keys with a final crash, but lingered,
as his fashion was when he had something to propose: if he felt pretty sure that the thing would be
liked, he brought it in as if he had only happened to
remember it. He now drew out a large, square, ceremo-
nious-looking envelope, at which he glanced as if, after
all, he was rather surprised to see it, and said, " Oh,
by the by, Mrs. Elmore, I wish you 'd tell me what to
do about this thing. Here 's something that 's come
to me in my official capacity, but it is n't exactly consular business, — if it was I don't believe I should
ask *any* lady for instructions, — and I don't know exactly what to do. It 's so long since I corresponded
with a princess that I don't even know how to answer her letter."

The ladies perhaps feared a hoax of some sort, and
would not ask to see the letter; and then Hoskins
recognized his failure to play upon their curiosity
with a laugh, and gave the letter to Mrs. Elmore.
It was an invitation to a mask ball, of which all
Venice had begun to speak. A great Russian lady,
who had come to spend the winter in the Lagoons,
and had taken a whole floor at one of the hotels, had

sent out her cards, apparently to all the available
people in the city, for the event which was to take
place a fortnight later.   In the mean time, a thrill of
preparation was felt in various quarters, and the ordinary course of life was interrupted in a way that gave
some idea of the old times, when Venice was the
capital of pleasure, and everything yielded there to
the great business of amusement.   Mrs. Elmore had
found it impossible to get a pair of fine shoes finished
until after the ball; a dress which Lily had ordered
could not be made; their laundress had given notice
that for the present all fluting and quilling was out
of the question; one already heard that the chief
Venetian perruquier and his assistants were engaged
for every moment of the forty-eight hours before the
ball, and that whoever had him now must sit up with
her hair dressed for two nights at least.   Mrs. Elmore
had a fanatical faith in these stories; and while
agreeing with her husband, as a matter of principle,
that mask balls were wrong, and that it was in bad
taste for a foreigner to insult the sorrow of Venice by
a festivity of the sort at such a time, she had secretly
indulged longings which the sight of Hoskins's invitation rendered almost insupportable.   Her longings
were not for herself, but for Lily: if she could provide Lily with the experience of a masquerade in

Venice, she could overpay all the kindnesses that the Mayhews had ever done her. It was an ambition neither ignoble nor ungenerous, and it was with a really heroic effort that she silenced it in passing the invitation to her husband, and simply saying to Hoskins, "Of course you will go."

"I don't know about that," he answered. "That's the point I want some advice on. You see this document calls for a lady to fill out the bill."

"Oh," returned Mrs. Elmore, "you will find some Americans at the hotels. You can take them."

"Well, now, I was thinking, Mrs. Elmore, that I should like to take you."

"Take me!" she echoed tremulously. "What an idea! I'm too old to go to mask balls."

"You don't look it," suggested Hoskins.

"Oh, I couldn't go," she sighed. "But it's very, very kind."

Hoskins dropped his head, and gave the low chuckle with which he confessed any little bit of humbug. "Well, you *or* Miss Lily."

Lily had retired to the other side of the room as soon as the parley about the invitation began. Without asking or seeing, she knew what was in the note, and now she felt it right to make a feint of not knowing what Mrs. Elmore meant when she asked, "What do *you* say, Lily?"

When the question was duly explained to her, she answered languidly, "I don't know. Do you think I'd better?"

"I might as well make a clean breast of it, first as last," said Hoskins. "I·thought perhaps Mrs. Elmore might refuse, she's so stiff about some things,"— here he gave that chuckle of his,— "and so I came prepared for contingencies. It occurred to me that it might n't be quite the thing, and so I went round to the Spanish consul and asked him how he thought it would do for me to matronize a young lady if I could get one, and he said he did n't think it would do at all." Hoskins let this adverse decision sink into the breasts of his listeners before he added : "But he said that he was going with his wife, and that if we would come along she could matronize us both. I don't know how it would work," he concluded impartially.

They all looked at Elmore, who stood holding the princess's missive in his hand, and darkly forecasting the chances of consent and denial. At the first suggestion of the matter, a reckless hope that this ball might bring Ehrhardt above their horizon again sprang up in his heart, and became a desperate fear when the whole responsibility of action was, as usual, left with him. He stood, feeling that Hoskins had used him very ill.

"I suppose," began Mrs. Elmore very thoughtfully, "that this will be something quite in the style of the old masquerades under the Republic."

"Regular Ridotto business, the Spanish consul says," answered Hoskins.

"It might be very useful to you, Owen," she resumed, "in an historical way, if Lily were to go and take notes of everything; so that when you came to that period you could describe its corruptions intelligently."

Elmore laughed. "I never thought of that, my dear," he said, returning the invitation to Hoskins. "Your historical sense has been awakened late, but it promises to be very active. Lily had better go, by all means, and I shall depend upon her coming home with very full notes upon her dance-list."

They laughed at the professor's sarcasm, and Hoskins, having undertaken to see that the last claims of etiquette were satisfied by getting an invitation sent to Miss Mayhew through the Spanish consul, went off, and left the ladies to the discussion of ways and means. Mrs. Elmore said that of course it was now too late to hope to get anything done, and then set herself to devise the character that Lily would have appeared in if there had been time to get her ready, or if all the work-people had not been so busy that it

was merely frantic to think of anything. She first
patriotically considered her as Columbia, with the
customary drapery of stars and stripes and the cap of
liberty. But while holding that she would have
looked very pretty in the dress, Mrs. Elmore decided
that it would have been too hackneyed; and besides,
everybody would have known instantly who it was.

"Why not have had her go in the character of
Mr. Hoskins's 'Westward'?" suggested Elmore, with
lazy irony.

"The very thing!" cried his wife. "Owen, you
deserve great credit for thinking of that; no one else
would have done it! No one will dream what it
means, and it will be great fun, letting them make
it out. We must keep it a dead secret from Mr.
Hoskins, and let her surprise him with it when he
comes for her that evening. It will be a very pretty
way of returning his compliment, and it will be a
sort of delicate acknowledgement of his kindness in
asking her, and in so many other ways. Yes, you've
hit it exactly, Owen; she shall go as 'Westward.'"

"Go?" echoed Elmore, who had with difficulty
realized the rapid change of tense. "I thought you
said you couldn't get her ready."

"We must manage somehow," replied Mrs. Elmore.
And somehow a shoemaker for the sandals, a seam-

stress for the delicate flowing draperies, a hair-dresser for the adjustment of the young girl's rebellious abundance of hair beneath the star-lit fillet, were actually found,—with the help of Hoskins, as usual, though he was not suffered to know anything of the character to whose make-up he contributed. The perruquier, a personage of lordly address naturally, and of a dignity heightened by the demand in which he found himself came early in the morning, and was received by Elmore with a self-possession that ill-comported with the solemnity of the occasion. "Sit down," said Elmore easily, pushing him a chair. "The ladies will be here presently."

"But I have no time to sit down, signore!" replied the artist, with an imperious bow, "and the ladies must be here instantly."

Mrs. Elmore always said that if she had not heard this conversation, and hurried in at once, the perruquier would have left them at that point. But she contrived to appease him by the manifestation of an intelligent sympathy ; she made Lily leave her breakfast untasted, and submit her beautiful head to the touch of this man, with whom it was but a head of hair and nothing more ; and in an hour the work was done. The artist whisked away the cloth which covered her shoulders, and crying, "Behold!" bowed splendidly

to the spectators, and without waiting for criticism or
suggestion, took his napoleon and went his way. All
that day the work of his skill was sacredly guarded,
and the custodian of the treasure went about with her
head on her shoulders, as if it had been temporarily
placed in her keeping, and were something she was
not at all used to taking care of. More than once
Mrs. Elmore had to warn her against sinister accidents.
" Remember, Lily," she said, " that if anything *did*
happen, NOTHING could be done to save you ! " In spite
of himself Elmore shared these anxieties, and in the
depths of his wonted studies he found himself pursued and harassed by vague apprehensions, which
upon analysis proved to be fears for Miss Lily's
hair. It was a great moment when the robe came
home — rather late — from the dressmaker's, and was
put on over Lily's head ; but from this thrilling rite
Elmore was of course excluded, and only knew of it
afterwards by hearsay. He did not see her till she
came out just before Hoskins arrived to fetch her
away, when she appeared radiantly perfect in her
dress, and in the air with which she meant to carry
it off. At Mrs. Elmore's direction she paraded daz-
zlingly up and down the room a number of times,
bending over to see how her dress hung, as she
walked. Mrs. Elmore, with her head on one side, scru-

tinized her in every detail, and Elmore regarded her young beauty and delight with a pride as innocent as her own. A dim regret, evaporating in a long sigh, which made the others laugh, recalled him to himself, as the bell rang and Hoskins appeared. He was received in a preconcerted silence, and he looked from one to the other with his queer, knowing smile, and took in the whole affair without a word.

"Is n't it a pretty idea?" said Mrs. Elmore. "Studied from an antique bas-relief, or just the same as an antique, — full of the anguish and the repose of the Laocoön."

"Mrs. Elmore," said the sculptor, "you 're too many for me. I reckon the procession had better start before I make a fool of myself. Well!" This was all Hoskins could say; but it sufficed. The ladies declared afterwards that if he had added a word more, it would have spoiled it. They had expected him to go to the ball in the character of a miner perhaps, or in that of a trapper of the great plains; but he had chosen to appear more naturally as a courtier of the time of Louis XIV. "When you go in for a disguise," he explained, "you can't make it too complete; and I consider that this limp of mine adds the last touch."

"It 's no use to sit up for them," Mrs. Elmore

said, when she and her husband had come in from calling good wishes and last instructions after them from the balcony, as their gondola pushed away. "We sha'n't see anything more of *them* till morning. Now this," she added, "is something like the gayety that people at home are always fancying in Europe. Why, I can remember when I used to imagine that American tourists figured brilliantly in *salons* and *conversazioni*, and spent their time in masking and throwing *confetti* in carnival, and going to balls and opera. I did n't know what American tourists were, then, and how dismally they moped about in hotels and galleries and churches. And I did n't know how stupid Europe was socially,— how perfectly dead and buried it was, especially for young people. It would be fun if things happened so that Lily never found it out! I don't think two offers already, — or three, if you count Rose-Black, — are very bad for *any* girl ; and now this ball, coming right on top of it, where she will see hundreds of handsome officers! Well, she 'll never miss Patmos, at this rate, will she ? "

"Perhaps she had better never have left Patmos," suggested Elmore gravely.

"I don't know what you mean, Owen," said his wife, as if hurt.

"I mean that it's a great pity she should give herself up to the same frivolous amusements here that
she had there. The only good that Europe can do
American girls who travel here is to keep them in
total exile from what they call a good time, — from
parties and attentions and flirtations; to force them,
through the hard discipline of social deprivation, to
take some interest in the things that make for civilization, — in history, in art, in humanity."

"Now, there I differ with you, Owen. I think
American girls are the nicest girls in the world, just
as they are. And I don't see any harm in the things
you think are so awful. You 've lived so long here
among your manuscripts that you 've forgotten there
is any such time as the present. If you are getting
so Europeanized, I think the sooner we go home the
better."

"*I* getting Europeanized!" began Elmore indignantly.

"Yes, Europeanized! And I don't want you to be
so severe with Lily, Owen. The child stands in terror
of you now; and if you keep on in this way, she can't
draw a natural breath in the house."

There is always something flattering, at first, to a
gentle and peaceable man in the notion of being
terrible to any one; Elmore melted at these words,

and at the fear that he might have been, in some way that he could not think of, really harsh.

"I should be very sorry to distress her," he began.

"Well, you have n't distressed her yet," his wife relented. "Only you must be careful not to. She was going to be very circumspect, Owen, on your account, for she really appreciates the interest you take in her, and I think she sees that it won't do to be at all free with strangers over here. This ball will be a great education for Lily,—a *great* education. I'm going to commence a letter to Sue about her costume, and all that, and leave it open to finish up when Lily gets home."

When she went to bed, she did not sleep till after the time when the girl ought to have come ; and when she awoke to a late breakfast, Lily had still not returned. By eleven o'clock she and Elmore had passed the stage of accusing themselves, and then of accusing each other, for allowing Lily to go in the way they had ; and had come to the question of what they had better do, and whether it was practicable to send to the Spanish consulate and ask what had become of her. They had resigned themselves to waiting for one half-hour longer, when they heard her voice at the water-gate, gayly forbidding Hoskins to come up ; and running out upon the balcony, Mrs. Elmore had a glimpse of the courtier, very tawdry by daylight, re-entering his gondola, and had only time to turn about when Lily burst laughing into the room.

"Oh, don't look at me, Professor Elmore!" she cried. "I'm literally danced to rags!"

Her dress and hair were splashed with drippings from the wax candles; she was wildly decorated with favors from the German, and one of these had been used to pin up a rent which the spur of a hussar had made in her robe; her hair had escaped from its fastenings during the night, and in putting it back she had broken the star in her fillet; it was now kept in place by a bit of black-and-yellow cord which an officer had lent her. "He said he should claim it of me the first time we met," she exclaimed excitedly. "Why, Professor Elmore," she implored with a laugh, "don't look at me *so!*"

Grief and indignation were in his heart. "You look like the spectre of last night," he said with dreamy severity, and as if he saw her merely as a vision.

"Why, that's the way I *feel!*" she answered; and with a reproachful "Owen!" his wife followed her flight to her room.

XI.

ELMORE went out for a long walk, from which he returned disconsolate at dinner. He was one of those people, common enough in our Puritan civilization, who would rather forego any pleasure than incur the reaction which must follow with all the keenness of remorse; and he always mechanically pitied (for the operation was not a rational one) such unhappy persons as he saw enjoying themselves. But he had not meant to add bitterness to the anguish which Lily would necessarily feel in retrospect of the night's gayety; he had not known that he was recognizing, by those unsparing words of his, the nervous misgivings in the girl's heart. He scarcely dared ask, as he sat down at table with Mrs. Elmore alone, whether Lily were asleep.

"Asleep?" she echoed, in a low tone of mystery. "I hope so."

"Celia, Celia!" he cried in despair. "What shall I do? I feel terribly at what I said to her."

"Sh! At what you said to her? Oh yes! Yes, that was cruel. But there is so much else, poor child, that I had forgotten that."

He let his plate of soup stand untasted. "Why — why," he faltered, "did n't she enjoy herself?" And a historian of Venice, whose mind should have been wholly engaged in philosophizing the republic's difficult past, hung abjectly upon the question whether a young girl had or had not had a good time at a ball.

"Yes. Oh, yes! She *enjoyed* herself — if that's all you require," replied his wife. "Of course she would n't have stayed so late if she had n't enjoyed herself."

"No," he said in a tone which he tried to make leading; but his wife refused to be led by indirect methods. She ate her soup, but in a manner to carry increasing bitterness to Elmore with every spoonful.

"Come, Celia!" he cried at last, "tell me what has happened. You know how wretched this makes me. Tell me it, whatever it is. Of course, I must know it in the end. Are there any new complications?"

"No *new* complications," said his wife, as if resenting the word. "But you make such a bugbear of the least little matter that there's no encouragement to tell you anything."

"Excuse me," he retorted, "I have n't made a bugbear of this."

"You have n't had the opportunity." This was so grossly unjust that Elmore merely shrugged his shoulders and remained silent. When it finally appeared that he was not going to ask anything more, his wife added: "If you could listen, like any one else, and not interrupt with remarks that distort all one's ideas"— Then, as he persisted in his silence, she relented still further. "Why, of course, as you say, you will have to know it in the end. But I can tell you, to begin with, Owen, that it's nothing you can do anything about, or take hold of in any way. Whatever it is, it's done and over; so it need n't distress you at all."

"Ah, I've known some things done and over that distressed me a great deal," he suggested.

"The princess was n't so very young, after all," said Mrs. Elmore, as if this had been the point in dispute, "but very fat and jolly, and very kind. She was n't in costume; but there was a young countess with her, helping receive, who appeared as Night, — black tulle, you know, with silver stars. The princess seemed to take a great fancy to Lily, — the Russians always *have* sympathized with us in the war, — and all the time she was n't dancing, the princess kept her by her, holding her hand and patting it. The officers — hundreds of them, in their white uniforms

and those magnificent hussar dresses — were very
obsequious to the princess, and Lily had only too
many partners. She says you can't imagine how
splendid the scene was, with all those different costumes, and the rooms a perfect blaze of waxlights;
the windows were battened, so that you could n't tell
when it came daylight, and she had n't any idea
how the time was passing. They were not all in
masks; and there did n't seem to be any regular hour
for unmasking. She can't tell just when the supper
was, but she thinks it must have been towards morning. She says Mr. Hoskins got on capitally, and
everybody seemed to like him, he was so jolly and
good-natured; and when they found out that he had
been wounded in the war, they made quite a belle of
him, as he called it. The princess made a point of
introducing all the officers to Lily that came up after
they unmasked. They paid her the greatest attention, and you can easily see that she was the prettiest girl there."

"I can believe that without seeing," said Elmore,
with magnanimous pride in the loveliness that had
made him so much trouble. "Well?"

"Well, they could n't any of them get the hang, as
Mr. Hoskins said, of the character she came in, for a
good while; but when they did, they thought it was

the best idea there : and it was all *your* idea, Owen,"
said Mrs. Elmore, in accents of such tender pride
that he knew she must now be approaching the difficult passage of her narration. " It was so perfectly
new and unconventional. She got on very well
speaking Italian with the officers, for she knew as
much of it as they did."

Here Mrs. Elmore paused, and glanced hesitatingly
at her husband. " They only made one little mistake ; but that was at the beginning, and they soon
got over it." Elmore suffered, but he did not ask
what it was, and his wife went on with smooth cau-
tion. " Lily thought it was just as it is at home, and
she must n't dance with any one unless they had
been introduced. So after the first dance with the
Spanish consul, as her escort, a young officer came
up and asked her ; and she refused, for she thought it
was a great piece of presumption. Afterwards the
princess told her she could dance with any one, introduced or not, and so she did ; and pretty soon she saw
this first officer looking at her very angrily, and going
about speaking to others and glancing toward her.
She felt badly about it, when she saw how it was ;
and she got Mr. Hoskins to go and speak to him.
Mr. Hoskins asked him if he spoke English, and the
officer said No ; and it seems that he did n't know

Italian either, and Mr. Hoskins tried him in Spanish,
— he picked up a little in New Mexico, — but the
officer did n't understand it; and all at once it occurred to Mr. Hoskins to say, ' Parlez-vous Français ? '
and says the officer instantly, ' Oui, monsieur.' "

" Of course the man knew French. He ought to
have tried him with that in the beginning. What
did Hoskins say then ? " asked Elmore impatiently.

" He did n't say anything : that was all the French
he knew."

Elmore broke into a cry of laughter, and laughed
on and on with the wild excess of a sad man when
once he unpacks his heart in that way. His wife did
not, perhaps, feel the absurdity as keenly as he, but
she gladly laughed with him, for it smoothed her way
to have him in this humor. " Mr. Hoskins just took
him by the arm, and said, ' Here ! you come along
with me,' and led him up to the princess, where Lily
was sitting ; and when the princess had explained to
him, Lily rose, and mustered up enough French to
say, 'Je vous prie, monsieur, de danser avec moi,' and
after that they were the greatest friends."

" That was very pretty in her ; it was sovereignly
gracious," said Elmore.

" Oh, if an American girl is left to manage for herself she can *always* manage ! " cried Mrs. Elmore.

"Well, and what else?" asked her husband.

"Oh, *I* don't know that it amounts to anything," said Mrs. Elmore; but she did not delay further.

It appeared from what she went on to say that in the German, which began not long after midnight, there was a figure fancifully called the symphony, in which musical toys were distributed among the dancers in pairs; the possessor of a small pandean pipe, or tin horn, went about sounding it, till he found some lady similarly equipped, when he demanded her in the dance. In this way a tall mask, to whom a penny trumpet had fallen, was stalking to and fro among the waltzers, blowing the silly plaything with a disgusted air, when Lily, all unconscious of him, where she sat with her hand in that of her faithful princess, breathed a responsive note. The mask was instantly at her side, and she was whirling away in the waltz. She tried to make him out, but she had already danced with so many people that she was unable to decide whether she had seen this mask before. He was not disguised except by the little visor of black silk, coming down to the point of his nose his blond whiskers escaped at either side, and his blond moustache swept beneath, like the whiskers and moustaches of fifty other officers present, and he did not speak. This was a permissible caprice of his but if she were resolved to make him speak, this also was a permissible caprice. She made a whole turn of the room in studying up the Italian sentence with which she assailed him : " Perdoni, Maschera ; ma cosa ha detto ?   Non ho ben inteso."

"Speak English, Mask," came the reply.   "I did not say anything."   It came certainly with a German accent, and with a foreigner's deliberation ; but it came at once, and clearly.

The English astonished her, and somehow it daunted her, for the mask spoke very gravely ; but she would not let him imagine that he had put her down, and she rejoined laughingly, " Oh, I knew that you had n't spoken, but I thought I would make you."

" You think you can make one do what you will ? " asked the mask.

" Oh, no.   I don't think I could make you tell me who you are, though I should like to make you."

" And why should you wish to know me ?   If you met me in Piazza, you would not recognize my salutation."

" How do you know that ? " demanded Lily.   " I don't know what you mean."

" Oh, it is understood yet already," answered the mask.   " Your compatriot, with whom you live, wishes to be well seen by the Italians, and he would not let you bow to an Austrian."

"That is not so," exclaimed Lily indignantly. "Professor Elmore would n't be so mean; and if he would, *I* should n't." She was frightened, but she felt her spirit rising, too. "You seem to know so well who I am : do you think it is fair for you to keep me in ignorance ? "

"I cannot remain masked without your leave. Shall I unmask ? Do you insist ? "

"Oh, no," she replied. " You will have to unmask at supper, and then I shall see you. I 'm not impatient. I prefer to keep you for a mystery."

" You will be a mystery to me even when you unmask," replied the mask gravely.

Lily was ill at ease, and she gave a little, unsuccessful laugh. " You seem to take the mystery very coolly," she said in default of anything else.

" I have studied the American manner," replied the mask. "In America they take everything coolly : life and death, love and hate — all things."

" How do you know that ? You have never been in America."

" That is not necessary, if the Americans come here to show us."

" They are not true Americans, if they show you that," cried the girl.

" No ? "

"But I see that you are only amusing yourself."

"And have you never amused yourself with me ?"

"How could I," she demanded, "if I never saw you before ? "

"But are you sure of that ?" She did not answer, for in this masquerade banter she had somehow been growing unhappy. "Shall I prove to you that you have seen me before ? You dare not let me unmask."

"Oh, I can wait till supper. I shall know then that I have never seen you before. I forbid you to unmask till supper! Will you obey ? " she cried anxiously.

"I have obeyed in harder things," replied the mask.

She refused to recognize anything but meaningless badinage in his words. "Oh, as a soldier, yes ! — you must be used to obeying orders." He did not reply, and she added, releasing her hand and slipping it into his arm, "I am tired now; will you take me back to the princess ? "

He led her silently to her place, and left her with a profound bow.

"Now," said the princess, "they shall give you a little time to breathe. I will not let them make you dance every minute. They are indiscreet. You shall not take any of their musical instruments, and so you can fairly escape till supper."

"Thank you," said Lily absently, "that will be the best way"; and she sat languidly watching the dancers. A young naval officer who spoke English ran across the floor to her.

"Come," he cried, "I shall have twenty duels on my hands if I let you rest here, when there are so many who wish to dance with you." He threw a pipe into her lap, and at the same moment a pipe sounded from the other side of the room.

"This is a conspiracy!" exclaimed the girl. "I will not have it! I am not going to dance any more." She put the pipe back into his hands; he placed it to his lips, and sounded it several times, and then dropped it into her lap again with a laugh, and vanished in the crowd.

"That little fellow is a rogue," said the princess. "But he is not so bad as some of them. Monsieur," she cried in French to the fair-whiskered, tall mask who had already presented himself before Lily, "I will not permit it, if it is for a trick. You must unmask. I will dispense mademoiselle from dancing with you."

The mask did not reply, but turned his eyes upon Lily with an appeal which the holes of the visor seemed to intensify. "It is a promise," she said to the princess, rising in a sort of fascination. "I have forbidden him to unmask before supper."

"Oh, very well," answered the princess, "if that is the case. But make him bring you back soon: it is almost time."

"Did you hear, Mask?" asked the girl, as they waltzed away. "I will only make two turns of the room with you."

"Perdoni?"

"This is too bad!" she exclaimed. "I will not be trifled with in this way. Either speak English, or unmask at once."

The mask again answered in Italian, with a repeated apology for not understanding. "You understand very well," retorted Lily, now really indignant, "and you know that this passes a jest."

"Can you speak German?" asked the mask in that tongue.

"Yes, a little, but I do not choose to speak it. If you have anything to say to me you can say it in English."

"I cannot understand English," replied the mask, still in German, and now Lily thought the voice seemed changed; but she clung to her belief that it was some hoax played at her expense, and she continued her efforts to make him answer her in English. The two turns round the room had stretched to half a dozen in this futile task, but she felt herself powerless to leave the mask, who for his part betrayed signs of embarrassment, as if he had undertaken a ruse of which he repented. A confused movement in the crowd and a sudden cessation of the music recalled her to herself, and she now took her partner's arm and hurried with him toward the place where she had left the princess. But the princess had already gone into the supper-room, and she had no other recourse than to follow with the stranger.

As they entered the supper-room she removed her little visor, and she felt, rather than saw, the mask put up his hand and lift away his own: he turned his head, and looked down upon her with the face of a man she had never seen before.

" Ah, you are there ! " she heard the princess's voice calling to her from one of the tables. " How tired you look ! Here — here ! I will make you drink this glass of wine."

The officer who brought her the wine gave her his arm and led her to the princess, and the late mask mixed with the two-score other tall blond officers.

The night which stretched so far into the day ended at last, and she followed Hoskins down to their gondola. He entered the boat first, to give her his hand in stepping from the *riva ;* at the same moment she involuntarily turned at the closing of the door behind her, and found at her side the tall blond mask, or one of the masks, if there were two who had danced with her. He caught her hand suddenly to his lips, and kissed it.

" Adieu — forgive ! " he murmured in English, and then vanished indoors again.

" Owen," said Mrs. Elmore dramatically at the end of her narration, " who do you think it could have been ? "

" I have no doubt as to who it was, Celia," replied Elmore, with a heat evidently quite unexpected to his wife, " and if Lily has not been seriously annoyed by the matter, I am glad that it has happened. I have had my regrets — my doubts — whether I did not dismiss that man's pretensions too curtly, too unkindly. But I am convinced now that we did exactly right, and that she was wise never to bestow another thought upon him. A man capable of contriving a petty persecution of this sort — of pursuing a young girl who had rejected him in this shameless fashion, — is no gentleman."

" It *was* a persecution," said Mrs. Elmore, with a dazed air, as if this view of the case had not occurred to her.

" A miserable, unworthy persecution ! " repeated her husband.

" Yes."

" And we are well rid of him. He has relieved *me* by this last performance, immensely ; and I trust that if Lily had any secret lingering regrets, he has given her a final lesson. Though I must say, in justice to her, poor girl, she did n't seem to need it."

Mrs. Elmore listened with a strange abeyance ; she looked beaten and bewildered, while he vehemently uttered these words. She could not meet his eyes, with her consciousness of having her intended romance thrown back upon her hands ; and he seemed in nowise eager to meet hers, for whatever consciousness of his own. " Well, it is n't certain that he was the one, after all," she said.

XII.

LONG after the ball Lily seemed to Elmore's eye not to have recovered her former tone. He thought she went about languidly, and that she was fitful and dreamy, breaking from moods of unwonted abstraction in bursts of gayety as unnatural. She did not talk much of the ball; he could not be sure that she ever recurred to it of her own motion. Hoskins continued to come a great deal to the house, and she often talked with him for a whole evening; Elmore fancied she was very serious in these talks.

He wondered if Lily avoided him, or whether this was only an illusion of his; but in any case, he was glad that the girl seemed to find so much comfort in Hoskins's company, and when it occurred to him he always said something to encourage his visits. His wife was singularly quiescent at this time, as if, having accomplished all she wished in Lily's presence at the princess's ball, she was willing to rest for a while from further social endeavor. Life was falling into the dull routine again, and after the past shocks his nerves were gratefully clothing themselves in the old habits of tranquillity once more, when one day a letter came from the overseers of Patmos University, offering him the presidency of that institution on condition of his early return. The board had in view certain changes, intended to bring the university abreast with the times, which they hoped would meet his approval.

Among these was a modification of the name, which was hereafter to be Patmos University and Military Institute. The board not only believed that popular feeling demanded the introduction of military drill into the college, but they felt that a college which had been closed at the beginning of the Rebellion, through the dedication of its president and nearly all its students to the war, could in no way so gracefully recognize this proud fact of its history as by hereafter making war one of the arts which it taught. The board explained that of course Mr. Elmore would not be expected to take charge of this branch of instruction at once. A competent military assistant would be provided, and continued under him as long as he should deem his services essential. The letter closed with a cordial expression of the desire of Elmore's old friends to have him once more in their midst, at the close of labors which they were sure would do credit to the good old university and to the whole city of Patmos.

Elmore read this letter at breakfast, and silently handed it to his wife : they were alone, for Lily, as now often happened, had not yet risen. "Well?" he said, when she had read it in her turn. She gave it back to him with a look in her dimmed eyes which he could not mistake. "I see there is no doubt of your feeling, Celia," he added.

"I don't wish to urge you," she replied, "but yes, I should like to go back. Yes, I am homesick. I have been afraid of it before, but this chance of returning makes it certain."

"And you see nothing ridiculous in my taking the presidency of a military institute?"

"They say expressly that they don't expect you to give instruction in that branch."

"No, not immediately, it seems," he said, with his pensive irony. "And the history?"

"Have n't you almost got notes enough?"

Elmore laughed sadly. "I have been here two years. It would take me twenty years to write such a history of Venice as I ought not to be ashamed to write ; it would take me five years to scamp it as I thought of doing. Oh, I dare say I had better go back. I have neither the time nor the money to give to a work I never was fit for, — of whose magnitude even I was unable to conceive."

"Don't say that!" cried his wife, with the old sympathy. "You will write it yet, I know you will. I would rather spend all my days in this — watery mausoleum than have you talk so, Owen!"

"Thank you, my dear; but the work won't be lost even if I give it up at this point. I can do something with my material, I suppose. And you know that if I did n't *wish* to give up my project I could n't. It's a sign of my unfitness for it that I'm able to abandon it. The man who is born to write the history of Venice will have no volition in the matter: he cannot leave it, and he will not die till he has finished it." He feebly crushed a bit of bread in his fingers as he ended with this burst of feeling, and he shook his head in sad negation to his wife's tender protest, — "Oh, you will come back some day to finish it!"

"No one ever comes back to finish a history of Venice," he said.

"Oh, yes, you will," she returned. "But you need the rest from this kind of work, now, just as you needed rest from your college work before. You need a change of standpoint, — and the American standpoint will be the very thing for you."

" Perhaps so, perhaps so," he admitted. " At any rate, this is a handsome offer, and most kindly made, Celia. It 's a great compliment. I did n't suppose they valued me so much."

" Of course they valued you, and they will be very glad to get you. I call it merely letting the historic material ripen in your mind, or else I should n't let you accept. And I shall be glad to go home, Owen, on Lily's account. The child is getting no good here: she 's drooping."

" Drooping ? "

" Yes. Don't you see how she mopes about ? "

" I 'm afraid — that — I have — noticed."

He was going to ask why she was drooping; but he could not. He said, recurring to the letter of the overseers, " So Patmos is a city."

" Of course it is by this time," said his wife, " with all that prosperity ! "

Now that they were determined to go, their little preparations for return were soon made; and a week after Elmore had written to accept the offer of the overseers, they were ready to follow his letter home. Their decision was a blow to Hoskins under which he visibly suffered; and they did not realize till then in what fond and affectionate friendship he held them. He now frankly spent his whole time with them ; he disconsolately helped them pack, and he did all that a consul can do to secure free entry for some objects of Venice that they wished to get in without payment of duties at New York.

He said a dozen times, "I don't know what I *will* do when you're gone"; and toward the last he alarmed them for his own interests by beginning to say, "Well, I don't see but what I will have to go along."

The last night but one Lily felt it her duty to talk to him very seriously about his future and what he owed to it. She told him that he must stay in Italy till he could bring home something that would honor the great, precious, suffering country for which he had fought so nobly, and which they all loved. She made the tears come into her eyes as she spoke, and when she said that she should always be proud to be associated with one of his works, Hoskins's voice was quite husky in replying: "Is that the way you feel about it ?" He went away promising to remain at least till he finished his bas-relief of Westward, and his figure of the Pacific Slope; and the next morning he sent around by a *facchino* a note to Lily.

She ran it through in the presence of the Elmores, before whom she received it, and then, with a cry of "I think Mr. Hoskins is too *bad !*" she threw it into Mrs. Elmore's lap, and, catching her handkerchief to her eyes, she broke into tears and went out of the room.   The note read : —·

DEAR MISS LILY, — Your kind interest in me gives me courage to say something that will very likely make me hateful to you forevermore. But I have got to say it, and you have got to know it; and it's all the worse for me if you have never suspected it. I want to give my whole life to you, wherever and however you will have it. With you by my side, I feel as if I could really do something that you would not be ashamed of in sculpture, and I believe that I could make you happy. I suppose I believe this because I love you very dearly, and I know the chances are that you will not think this is reason enough. But I would take one chance in a million, and be only too glad of it. I hope it will not worry you to read this: as I said before, I had to tell you. Perhaps it won't be altogether a surprise. I might go on, but I suppose that until I hear from you I had better give you as little of my eloquence as possible.

CLAY HOSKINS.

"Well, upon my word," said Elmore, to whom his wife had transferred the letter, "this is very indelicate of Hoskins!   I must say, I expected something better of him."   He looked at the note with a face of disgust.

"I don't know why you had a right to expect anything better of him, as you call it," retorted his wife.   "It's perfectly natural."

"Natural!" cried Elmore. "To put this upon us at the last moment, when he knows how much trouble I've ——"

Lily re-entered the room as precipitately as she had left it, and saved him from betraying himself as to the extent of his confidences to Hoskins. "Professor Elmore," she said, bending her reddened eyes upon him, "I want you to answer this letter for me; and I don't want you to write as you— I mean, don't make it so cutting — so — so — Why, I *like* Mr. Hoskins! He's been so *kind!* And if you said anything to wound his feelings —"

"I shall not do that, you may be sure; because, for one reason, I shall say nothing at all to him," replied Elmore.

"You won't write to him?" she gasped.

"No."

"Why, what shall I do-o-o-o?" demanded Lily, prolonging the syllable in a burst of grief and astonishment.

"I don't know," answered Elmore.

"Owen," cried his wife, interfering for the first time, in response to the look of appeal that Lily turned upon her, "you *must* write!"

"Celia," he retorted boldly, "I *won't* write. I have a genuine regard for Hoskins; I respect him, and I

am very grateful to him for all his kindness to you.
He has been like a brother to you both."

"Why, of course," interrupted Lily, "I never
thought of him as anything *but* a brother."

"And though I must say I think it would have
been more thoughtful and — and — more considerate
in him not to do this — "

"We did everything we could to fight him off from
it," interrupted Mrs. Elmore, "both of us. We saw
that it was coming, and we tried to stop it. But
nothing would help. Perhaps, as he says, he *did*
have to do it."

"I did n't dream of his — having any such — idea,"
said Elmore. "I felt so perfectly safe in his coming;
I trusted everything to him."

"I suppose you thought his wanting to come was
all unconscious cerebration," said his wife disdain-
fully. "Well, now you see it was n't."

"Yes; but it 's too late now to help it; and though
I think he ought to have spared us this, if he thought
there was no hope for him, still I can't bring myself
to inflict pain upon him, and the long and the short of
it is, I *won 't.*"

"But how is he to be answered ?"

"I don 't know. *You* can answer him."

"I could never do it in the world !"

"I own it's difficult," said Elmore coldly.

"Oh, *I* will answer him — I will answer him," cried Lily, "rather than have any trouble about it. Here, — here," she said, reaching blindly for pen and paper, as she seated herself at Elmore's desk, "give me the ink, quick. Oh, dear! What shall I say? What date is it? — the 25th? And it does n't matter about the day of the week. 'Dear Mr. Hoskins — Dear Mr. Hoskins — Dear Mr. Hosk' — Ought you to put Clay Hoskins, Esq., at the top or the bottom — or not at all, when you've said Dear Mr. Hoskins? Esquire seems so cold, anyway, and I *won't* put it! 'Dear Mr. Hoskins' — Professor Elmore!" she implored reproachfully, "tell me what to say!"

"That would be equivalent to writing the letter," he began.

"Well, write it, then," she said, throwing down the pen. "I don't *ask* you to dictate it. Write it, — write anything, — just in pencil, you know; that won't commit you to anything; they say a thing in pencil is n't legal, — and I'll copy it out in the first person."

"Owen," said his wife, "you shall not refuse! It's inhuman, it's inhospitable, when Lily wants you to, so! Why, I never heard of such a thing!"

Elmore desperately caught up the sheet of paper on

which Lily had written "Dear Mr. Hoskins," and groaning out "Well, well!" he added,—

I have your letter. Come to the station to-morrow and say good-by to her whom you will yet live to thank for remaining only   Your friend,

ELIZABETH MAYHEW.

"There! there, that will do beautifully — beautifully! Oh, thank you, Professor Elmore, ever and ever so much! That will save his feelings, and do everything," said Lily, sitting down again to copy it; while Mrs. Elmore, looking over her shoulder, mingled her hysterical excitement with the girl's, and helped her out by sealing the note when it was finished and directed.

It accomplished at least one purpose intended. It kept Hoskins away till the final moment, and it brought him to the station for their adieux just before their train started. A consciousness of the absurdity of his part gave his face a humorously rueful cast. But he came pluckily to the mark. He marched straight up to the girl. "It 's all right, Miss Lily," he said, and offered her his hand, which she had a strong impulse to cry over. Then he turned to Mrs. Elmore, and while he held her hand in his right, he placed his left affectionately on Elmore's shoulder, and, looking at Lily, he said, "You ought to get Miss Lily to help you out with your history, Professor; she has a very good style, — quite a literary style, I should have said, if I had n't known it was hers. I don't like her subjects, though." They broke into a forlorn laugh together; he wrung their hands once more, without a word, and, without looking back, limped out of the waiting-room and out of their lives.

They did not know that this was really the last of Hoskins, — one never knows that any parting is the last, — and in their inability to conceive of a serious passion in him, they quickly consoled themselves for what he might suffer. They knew how kindly, how tenderly even, they felt towards him, and by that juggle with the emotions which we all practise at times, they found comfort for him in the fact. Another interest, another figure, began to occupy the morbid fancy of Elmore, and as they approached Peschiera his expectation became intense. There was no reason why it should exist; it would be by the thousandth chance, even if Ehrhardt were still there, that they should meet him at the railroad station, and there were a thousand chances that he was no longer in Peschiera. He could see that his wife and Lily were restive too : as the train drew into the station they nodded to each other, and pointed out of the window, as if to identify the spot where

Lily had first noticed him; they laughed nervously, and it seemed to Elmore that he could not endure their laughter.

During that long wait which the train used to make in the old Austrian times at Peschiera, while the police authorities *viséd* the passports of those about to cross the frontier, Elmore continued perpetually alert. He was aware that he should not know Ehrhardt if he met him; but he should know that he was present from the looks of Lily and Mrs. Elmore, and he watched them. They dined well in waiting, while he impatiently trifled with the food, and ate next to nothing; and they calmly returned to their places in the train, to which he remounted after a last despairing glance around the platform in a passion of disappointment. The old longing not to be left so wholly to the effect of what he had done possessed him to the exclusion of all other sensations, and as the train moved away from the station he fell back against the cushions of the carriage, sick that he should never even have looked on the face of the man in whose destiny he had played so fatal a part.

XIII.

In America, life soon settled into form about the daily duties of Elmore's place, and the daily pleasures and cares which his wife assumed as a leader in Patmos society. Their sojourn abroad conferred its distinction; the day came when they regarded it as a brilliant episode, and it was only by fitful glimpses that they recognized its essential dulness. After they had been home a year or two, Elmore published his Story of Venice in the Lives of her Heroes, which fell into a ready oblivion; he paid all the expenses of the book, and was puzzled that, in spite of this, the final settlement should still bring him in debt to his publishers. He did not understand, but he submitted; and he accepted the failure of his book very meekly. If he could have chosen, he would have preferred that the Saturday Review, which alone noticed it in London with three lines of exquisite slight, should have passed it in silence. But after

all, he felt that the book deserved no better fate. He
always spoke of it as unphilosophized and incom-
plete, without any just claim to being.

Lily had returned to her sister's household, but
though she came home in the heyday of her young
beauty, she failed somehow to take up the story of
her life just where she had left it in Patmos. On the
way home she had refused an offer in London, and
shortly after her arrival in America she received a
letter from a young gentleman whom she had casu-
ally seen in Geneva, and who had found exile insupportable since parting with her, and was ready to
return to his native land at her bidding; but she said
nothing of these proposals till long afterwards to
Professor Elmore, who, she said, had suffered enough
from her offers. She went to all the parties and
picnics, and had abundant opportunities of flirtation
and marriage; but she neither flirted nor married.
She seemed to have greatly sobered; and the sound
sense which she had always shown became more
and more qualified with a thoughtful sweetness. At
first, the relation between her and the Elmores lost
something of its intimacy; but when, after several
years, her health gave way, a familiarity, even kinder
than before, grew up. She used to like to come to
them, and talk and laugh fondly over their old Vene-

tian days. But often she sat pensive and absent, in the midst of these memories, and looked at Elmore with a regard which he found hard to bear: a gentle, unconscious wonder it seemed, in which he imagined a shade of tender reproach.

When she recovered her health, after a journey to the West one winter, they saw that, by some subtile and indefinable difference, she was no longer a young girl. Perhaps it was because they had not met her for half a year. But perhaps it was age, — she was now thirty. However it was, Elmore recognized with a pang that the first youth at least had gone out of her voice and eyes. She only returned to arrange for a long sojourn in the West. She liked the climate and the people, she said; and she seemed well and happy. She had planned starting a Kindergarten school in Omaha with another young lady; she said that she wanted something to do. "She will end by marrying one of those Western widowers," said Mrs. Elmore.

"I wonder she did n't take poor old Hoskins," mused Elmore aloud.

"No, you don't, dear," said his wife, who had not grown less direct in dealing with him. "You know it would have been ridiculous; besides, she never cared anything for him, — she could n't. You might

as well wonder why she did n't take Captain Ehrhardt
after you dismissed him."

"*I* dismissed him ? "

" You wrote to him, did n't you ? "

" Celia," cried Elmore, "this I *cannot* bear. Did
I take a single step in that business without her
request and your full approval? Did n't you both
ask me to write?"

" Yes, I suppose we did."

" Suppose ? "

"Well, we *did*, — if you want me to say it. And
I 'm not accusing you of anything. I know you
acted for the best. But you can see yourself, can't
you, that it was rather sudden to have it end so
quickly — "

She did not finish her sentence, or he did not hear
the close in the miserable absence into which he
lapsed. "Celia," he asked at last, "do you think
she — she had any feeling about him ?"

"Oh," cried his wife restively, "how should *I*
know ? "

"I did n't suppose you *knew*," he pleaded. "I
asked if you thought so."

"What would be the use of thinking anything
about it ? The matter can't be helped now. If you
inferred from anything she said to you — "

"She told me repeatedly, in answer to questions as explicit as I could make them, that she wished him dismissed."

"Well, then, very likely she did."

"Very likely, Celia?"

"Yes. At any rate, it's too late now."

"Yes, it's too late now." He was silent again, and he began to walk the floor, after his old habit, without speaking. He was always mute when he was in pain, and he startled her with the anguish in which he now broke forth. "I give it up! I give it up! Celia, Celia, I'm afraid I did wrong! Yes, I'm afraid that I spoiled two lives. I ventured to lay my sacrilegious hands upon two hearts that a divine force was drawing together, and put them asunder. It was a lamentable blunder, — it was a crime!"

"Why, Owen, how strangely you talk! How could you have done any differently under the circumstances?"

"Oh, I could have done very differently. I might have seen him, and talked with him brotherly, face to face. He was a fearless and generous soul! And I was meanly scared for my wretched little decorums, for my responsibility to her friends, and I gave him no chance."

"We would n't let you give him any," interrupted his wife.

"Don't try to deceive yourself, don't try to deceive *me*, Celia! I know well enough that you would have been glad to have me show mercy; and I would not even show him the poor grace of passing his offer in silence, if I must refuse it. I could n't spare him even so much as that!"

"We decided — we both decided — that it would be better to cut off all hope at once," urged his wife.

"Ah, it was I who decided that — decided everything. Leave me to deal honestly with myself at last, Celia! I have tried long enough to believe that it was not I who did it!" The pent-up doubt of years, the long-silenced self-accusal, burst forth in his words. "Oh, I have suffered for it! I thought he must come back, somehow, as long as we stayed in Venice. When we left Peschiera without a glimpse of him — I wonder I outlived it. But even if I had seen him there, what use would it have been? Would I have tried to repair the wrong done? What did I do but impute unmanly and impudent motives to him when he seized his chance to see her once more at that masquerade — "

"No, no, Owen! He was not the one. Lily was satisfied of that long ago. It was nothing but a chance, a coincidence. Perhaps it was some one he had told about the affair — "

"No matter! no matter! If I thought it was he, my blame is the same. And she, poor girl, — in my lying compassion for him, I used to accuse her of cold-heartedness, of indifference! I wonder she did not abhor the sight of me. How has she ever tolerated the presence, the friendship, of a man who did her this irreparable wrong? Yes, it has spoiled her life, and it was my work. No, no, Celia! you and she had nothing to do with it, except as I forced your consent — it was my work; and, however I have tried openly and secretly to shirk it, I must bear this fearful responsibility."

He dropped into a chair, and hid his face in his hands, while his wife soothed him with loving excuses for what he had done, with tender protests against the exaggerations of his remorse. She said that he had done the only thing he could do; that Lily wished it, and that she never had blamed him. "Why, I don't believe she would ever have married Captain Ehrhardt, anyhow. She was full of that silly fancy of hers about Dick Burton, all the time, —you know how she used always to be talking about him; and when she came home and found she had outgrown him, she had to refuse him, and I suppose it's that that's made her rather melancholy." She explained that Major Burton had become extremely fat, that his moustache was too big and black, and his laugh too loud; there was nothing left of him, in fact, but his empty sleeve, and Lily was too conscientious to marry him merely for that.

In fact, Elmore's regret did reflect a monstrous and distorted image of his conduct. He had really acted the part of a prudent and conscientious man; he was perfectly justifiable at every step: but in the retrospect those steps which we can perfectly justify sometimes seem to have cost so terribly that we look back even upon our sinful stumblings with better heart. Heaven knows how such things will be at the last day; but at that moment there was no wrong, no folly of his youth, of which Elmore did not think with more comfort than of this passage in which he had been so wise and right.

Of course the time came when he saw it all differently again; when his wife persuaded him that he had done the best that any one could do with the responsibilities that ought never to have been laid on a man of his temperament and habits; when he even came to see that Lily's feeling was a matter of pure conjecture with him, and that so far as he knew she had never cared anything for Ehrhardt. Yet he was glad to have her away; he did not like to talk of her with his wife; he did not think of her if he could help it.

They heard from time to time through her sister
that her little enterprise in Omaha was prospering,
and that she was very contented out West; at last
they heard directly from her that she was going to
be married. Till then, Elmore had been dumbly tor-
mented in his sombre moods with the solution of a
problem at which his imagination vainly toiled, —
the problem of how some day she and Ehrhardt
should meet again and retrieve the error of the past
for him. He contrived this encounter in a thousand different ways by a thousand different chances;
what he so passionately and sorrowfully longed for
accomplished itself continually in his dreams, but
only in his dreams.

In due course Lily married, and from all they could
understand, very happily. Her husband was a clergy-
man, and she took particular interest in his parochial
work, which her good heart and clear head especially
qualified her to share with him. To connect her fate
any longer with that of Ehrhardt was now not only
absurd, it was improper ; yet Elmore sometimes found
his fancy forgetfully at work as before. He could not
at once realize that the tragedy of this romance, such
as it was, remained to him alone, except perhaps as
Ehrhardt shared it. With him, indeed, Elmore still
sought to fret his remorse and keep it poignant, and

his final failure to do so made him ashamed. But
what lasting sorrow can one have from the disappointment of a man whom one has never seen? If
Lily could console herself, it seemed probable that
Ehrhardt too had "got along."

AT THE SIGN OF THE SAVAGE.

AT THE SIGN OF THE SAVAGE.

As they bowled along in the deliberate German express train through the Black Forest, Colonel Kenton said he had only two things against the region: it was not black, and it was not a forest. He had all his life heard of the Black Forest, and he hoped he knew what it was. The inhabitants burned charcoal, high up the mountains, and carved toys in the winter when shut in by the heavy snows; they had Easter eggs all the year round, with overshot mill-wheels in the valleys, and cherry-trees all about, always full of blossoms or ripe fruit, just as you liked to think. They were very poor people, but very devout, and lived in little villages on a friendly intimacy with their cattle. The young women of these hamlets had each a long braid of yellow hair down her back, blue eyes, and a white bodice with a cat's-cradle lacing behind; the men had bell-crowned hats and spindle-legs: they buttoned the breath out of their bodies with round pewter buttons on tight, short crimson waistcoats.

"Now, here," said the colonel, breathing on the window of the car and rubbing a little space clear of the frost, "I see nothing of the sort. Either I have been imposed upon by what I have heard of the Black Forest, or this is not the Black Forest. I'm inclined to believe that there is no Black Forest, and never was. There is n't," he added, looking again, so as not to speak hastily, "a charcoal-burner, or an Easter egg, or a cherry blossom, or a yellow braid, or a red waistcoat, to enliven the whole desolate landscape. What are we to think of it, Bessie?"

Mrs. Kenton, who sat opposite, huddled in speechless comfort under her wraps and rugs, and was just trying to decide in her own mind whether it was more delicious to let her feet, now that they were thoroughly warm, rest upon the carpet-covered cylinder of hot water, or hover just a hair's breadth above it without touching it, answered a little impatiently that she did not know. In ordinary circumstances she would not have been so short with the colonel's nonsense. She thought that was the way all men talked when they got well acquainted with you; and, as coming from a sex incapable of seriousness, she could have excused it if it had not interrupted her in her solution of so nice a problem. Colonel Kenton, however, did not mind. He at once possessed himself of much more than his share of the cylinder, extorting a cry of indignation from his wife, who now saw herself reduced from a fastidious choice of luxuries to a mere vulgar strife for the necessaries of life, — a thing any woman abhors.

"Well, well," said the colonel, "keep your old hot-water bottle. If there was any other way of warming my feet, I would n't touch it. It makes me sick to use it; I feel as if the doctor was going to order me some boneset tea. Give *me* a good red-hot patent car-heater, that smells enough of burning iron to make your head ache in a minute, and sets your car on fire as soon as it rolls over the embankment. That's what *I* call comfort. A hot-water bottle shoved under your feet — I should suppose I *was* a woman, and a feeble one at that. I 'll tell you what *I* think about this Black Forest business, Bessie : I think it's part of a system of deception that runs through the whole German character. I have heard the Germans praised for their sincerity and honesty, but I tell you they have got to work hard to convince me of it, from this out. I am on my guard. I am not going to be taken in any more."

It became the colonel's pleasure to develop and ex-

emplify this idea at all points of their progress through
Germany. They were going to Italy, and as Mrs.
Kenton had had enough of the sea in coming to
Europe, they were going to Italy by the only all-rail
route then existing, — from Paris to Vienna, and so
down through the Simmering to Trieste and Venice.
Wherever they stopped, whatever they did before
reaching Vienna, Colonel Kenton chose to preserve
his guarded attitude. "Ah, they pretend this is
Stuttgart, do they?" he said on arriving at the
Suabian capital. "A likely story! They pretended
that was the Black Forest, you know, Bessie." At
Munich, "And this is Munich!" he sneered, whenever the conversation flagged during their sojourn.
"It's outrageous, the way they let these swindling
little towns palm themselves off upon the traveller for
cities he's heard of. This place will be calling itself
Berlin, next." When his wife, guide-book in hand,
was struggling to heat her admiration at some cold
history of Kaulbach, and in her failure clinging fondly
to the fact that Kaulbach had painted it, "Kaulbach!" the colonel would exclaim, and half close his
eyes and slowly nod his head and smile. "What
guide-book is that you've got, Bessie?" looking curiously at the volume he knew so well. "Oh! —
Baedeker! And are you going to let a Black Forest

Dutchman like Baedeker persuade you that this daub is by Kaulbach? Come! That's a little too much!" He rejected the birthplaces of famous persons one and all; they could not drive through a street or into a park, whose claims to be this or that street or park he did not boldly dispute; and he visited a pitiless incredulity upon the dishes of the *table d'hôte*, concerning which he always answered his wife's questions: "Oh, he *says* it's beef," or veal, or fowl, as the case might be; and though he never failed to relish his own dinner, strange fears began to affect the appetite of Mrs. Kenton. It happened that he never did come out with these sneers before other travellers, but his wife was always expecting him to do so, and afterwards portrayed herself as ready to scream, the whole time. She was not a nervous person, and regarding the colonel's jokes as part of the matrimonial contract, she usually bore them, as I have hinted, with severe composure; accepting them all, good, bad, and indifferent, as something in the nature of man which she should understand better after they had been married longer. The present journey was made just after the close of the war; they had seen very little of each other while he was in the army, and it had something of the fresh interest of a bridal tour. But they sojourned only a day or two in the places

between Strasburg and Vienna ; it was very cold and
very unpleasant getting about, and they instinctively
felt what every wise traveller knows, that it is folly to
be lingering in Germany when you can get into Italy;
and so they hurried on.

It was nine o'clock one night when they reached
Salzburg ; and when their baggage had been visited
and their passports examined, they had still half an
hour to wait before the train went on. They profited
by the delay to consider what hotel they should stop
at in Vienna, and they advised with their Bradshaw
on the point. This railway guide gave in its laconic
fashion several hotels, and specified the Kaiserin Elisabeth as one at which there was a table d'hôte, briefly
explaining that at most hotels in Vienna there was
none.

"That settles it," said Mrs. Kenton. "We will go
to the Kaiserin Elisabeth, of course. I'm sure I
never want the bother of ordering dinner in English,
let alone German, which never was meant for human
beings to speak."

"It's a language you can't tell the truth in," said
the colonel thoughtfully. "You can't call an open
country an open country ; you have to call it a Black
Forest." Mrs. Kenton sighed patiently. "But I don't
know about this Kaiserin Elisabeth business. How

do we know that's the *real* name of the hotel? How can *we* be sure that it isn't an *alias*, an assumed name, trumped up for the occasion? I tell you, Bessie, we can't be too cautious as long as we're in this fatherland of lies. What guide-book is this? Baedeker? Oh! Bradshaw. Well, that's some comfort. Bradshaw's an Englishman, at least. If it had been Baedeker" —

"Oh, Edward, Edward!" Mrs. Kenton burst out. "Will you *never* give that up? Here you've been harping on it for the last four days, and worrying my life out with it. I think it's unkind. It's perfectly bewildering me. I don't know where or what I am, any more." Some tears of vexation started to her eyes, at which Colonel Kenton put the shaggy arm of his overcoat round her, and gave her an honest hug.

"Well," he said, "I give it up, from this out. Though I shall always say that it was a joke that wore well. And I can tell you, Bessie, that it's no small sacrifice to give up a joke that you've just got into prime working order, so that you can use it on almost anything that comes up. But that's a thing that you can never understand. Let it all pass. We'll go to the Kaiserin Elisabeth, and submit to any sort of imposition they've a mind to practise upon us. I shall not breathe freely, I suppose, till we get into Italy, where people mean what they say. Haw, haw, haw!" laughed the colonel, "honest Iago's the man *I'm* after."

The doors of the waiting-room were thrown open, and cries of "Erste Klasse! Zweite Klasse! Dritte Klasse!" summoned the variously assorted passengers to carriages of their several degrees. The colonel lifted his little wife into a non-smoking first-class carriage, and established her against the cushioned barrier dividing the two seats, so that her feet could just reach the hot-water bottle, as he called it, and tucked her in and built her up so with wraps that she was a prodigy of comfort; and then folding about him the long fur-lined coat which she had bought him at Munich (in spite of his many protests that the fur was artificial), he sat down on the seat opposite, and proudly enjoyed the perfect content that beamed from Mrs. Kenton's face, looking so small from her heap of luxurious coverings.

"Well, Bessie, this would be very pleasant — if you could believe in it," he said, as the train smoothly rolled out of the station. "But of course it can't be genuine. There must be some dodge about it. I've no doubt you'll begin to feel perfectly horrid, the first thing you know."

Mrs. Kenton let him go on, as he did at some length, and began to drowse, while he amused himself with a gross parody of things she had said during the past four days. In those years while their wedded bliss was yet practically new, Colonel Kenton found his wife an inexhaustible source of mental refreshment. He prized beyond measure the feminine inadequacy and excess of her sayings; he had stored away such a variety of these that he was able to talk her personal parlance for an hour together; indeed, he had learned the trick of inventing phrases so much in her manner that Mrs. Kenton never felt quite safe in disowning any monstrous thing attributed to her. Her drowse now became a little nap, and presently a·delicious doze, in which she drifted far away from actual circumstance into a realm where she seemed to exist as a mere airy thought of her physical self; suddenly she lost this thought, and slept through all stops at stations and all changes of the hot-water cylinder, to renew which the guard, faithful to Colonel Kenton's bribe, alone opened the door.

"Wake up, Bessie!" she heard her husband saying. "We're at Vienna."

It seemed very improbable, but she did not dispute it. "What time is it?" she asked, as she suffered herself to be lifted from the carriage into the keen air of the winter night.

"Three o'clock," said the colonel, hurrying her into the waiting-room, where she sat, still somewhat remote from herself but getting nearer and nearer, while he went off about the baggage. "Now, then!" he cried cheerfully when he returned; and he led his wife out and put her into a *fiacre*. The driver bent from his perch and arrested the colonel, as he was getting in after Mrs. Kenton, with words in themselves unintelligible, but so probably in demand for neglected instructions that the colonel said, "Oh! Kaiserin Elisabeth!" and again bowed his head towards the fiacre door, when the driver addressed further speech to him, so diffuse and so presumably unnecessary that Colonel Kenton merely repeated, with rising impatience, "Kaiserin Elisabeth, — Kaiserin Elisabeth, I tell you!" and getting in shut the fiacre door after him.

The driver remained a moment in mumbled soliloquy; then he smacked his whip and drove rapidly away. They were aware of nothing outside but the starlit winter morning in unknown streets, till they plunged at last under an archway and drew up at a sort of lodge door, from which issued an example of the universal gold-cap-banded continental hotel *portier*, so like all others in Europe that it seemed idle for him to be leading an individual existence. He took the colonel's passport and summoned a waiter, who went bowing before them up a staircase more or less grandiose, and led them to a pleasant chamber, whither he sent directly a woman servant. She bade them a hearty good morning in her tongue, and, kneeling down before the tall porcelain stove, kindled from her apronful of blocks and sticks a fire that soon penetrated the travellers with a rich comfort. It was of course too early yet to think of breakfast, but it was fortunately not too late to think of sleep. They were both very tired, and it was almost noon when they woke. The colonel had the fire rekindled, and he ordered breakfast to be served them in their room. " Beefsteak and coffee — here ! " he said, pointing to the table ; and as he made Mrs. Kenton snug near the stove he expatiated in her own terms upon the perfect loveliness of the whole affair, and the touch of nature that made coffee and beefsteak the same in every language. It seemed that the Kaiserin Elisabeth knew how to serve such a breakfast in faultless taste ; and they sat long over it, in that sense of sovereign satisfaction which beefsteak and coffee in your own room can best give. At last the colonel rose briskly and announced the order of the day. They were to go here, they were to stop there ; they were to see this, they were to do that.

"Nothing of the kind," said Mrs. Kenton. "I am not going out at all to-day. It's too cold; and if we are to push on to Trieste to-morrow, I shall need the whole day to get a little rested. Besides, I have some jobs of mending to do that can't be put off any longer."

The colonel listened with an air of joyous admiration. "Bessie," said he, "this is inspiration. *I* don't want to see their old town; and I shall ask nothing better than to spend the day with you here at our own fireside. You can sew, and I — I'll *read* to you, Bessie!" This was a little too gross; even Mrs. Kenton laughed at this, the act of reading being so abhorrent to Colonel Kenton's active temperament that he was notorious for his avoidance of all literature except newspapers. In about ten minutes, passed in an agreeable idealization of his purpose, which came in that time to include the perusal of all the books on Italy he had picked up on their journey, the colonel said he would go down and ask the portier if they had the New York papers.

When he returned, somewhat disconsolate, to say they had not, and had apparently never heard of the Herald or Tribune, his wife smiled subtly: "Then I suppose you 'll have to go to the consul's for them."

"Why, Bessie, it is n't a thing I should have suggested ; I can't bear the thoughts of leaving you here alone ; but as you *say !* No, I 'll tell you : I 'll not go for the New York papers, but I will just step round and call upon the representative of the country — pay my respects to him, you know -- if you *wish* it. But I 'd far rather spend the time here with you, Bessie, in our cosy little boudoir ; I would, indeed."

Mrs. Kenton now laughed outright, and — it was a tremendous sarcasm for her — asked him if he were not afraid the example of the Black Forest was becoming infectious.

" Oh, come now, Bessie ; no joking," pleaded the colonel, in mock distress. " I 'll tell you what, my dear, the head waiter here speaks English like a — an Ollendorff ; and if you get to feeling a little lonesome while I 'm out, you can just ring and order something from him, you know. It will cheer you up to hear the sound of your native tongue in a foreign land. But, pshaw ! *I* sha 'nt be gone a minute ! "

By this time the colonel had got on his overcoat and gloves, and had his hat in one hand, and was leaning over his wife, resting the other hand on the back of the chair in which she sat warming the toes of her slippers at the draft of the stove. She popped him a cheery little kiss on his mustache, and gave

him a small push : " Stay as long as you like, Ned. I
shall not be in the least lonesome. I shall do my
mending, and then I shall take a nap, and by that
time it will be dinner. You need n't come back
before dinner. What hour is the table d'hôte ? "

" Oh ! " cried the colonel guiltily. " The fact is, I
was n't going to tell you, I thought it would vex you
so much : there *is* no table d'hôte here and never was.
Bradshaw has been depraved by the moral atmos-
phere of Germany. I 'd as soon trust Baedeker after
this."

" Well, never mind," said Mrs. Kenton. " We can
tell them to bring us what they like for dinner, and
we can have it whenever *we* like."

" Bessie ! " exclaimed the colonel, " I have not
done justice to you, and I supposed I had. I knew
how bright and beautiful you were, but I *did n't*
think you were so amiable. I did n't, indeed. This
is a real surprise," he said, getting out at the door.
He opened it to add that he would be back in an
hour, and then he went his way, with the light heart
of a husband who has a day to himself with his wife's
full approval.

At the consulate a still greater surprise awaited
Colonel Kenton. This was the consul himself, who
proved to be an old companion-in-arms, and into

whose awful presence the colonel was ushered by a
Hausmeister in a cocked hat and a gold-braided uniform finer than that of all the American major-
generals put together.   The friends both shouted
" Hollo ! " and " *You* don't say so ! " and threw back
their heads and laughed.

"Why, did n't you know I was here ? " demanded
the consul when the hard work of greeting was over.
" I thought everybody knew that."

" Oh, I knew you were rusting out in some of these
Dutch towns, but I never supposed it was Vienna.
But that does n't make any difference, so long as you
are here."   At this they smacked each other on the
knees, and laughed again.   That carried them by a
very rough point in their astonishment, and they now
composed themselves to the pleasure of telling each
other how they happened to be then and there, with
glances at their personal history when they were
making it together in the field.

" Well, now, what are you going to do the rest of
the day ? " asked the consul at last, with a look at his
watch.   " As I understand it, you 're going to spend
it with me, somehow.   The question is, how would
you like to spend it ? "

" This is a handsome offer, Davis ; but I don't see
how I 'm to manage exactly," replied the colonel, for

the first time distinctly recalling the memory of Mrs. Kenton. " My wife would n't know what had become of me, you know."

" Oh, yes, she would," retorted the consul, with a bachelor's ignorant ease of mind on a point of that kind. " We 'll go round and take her with us."

The colonel gravely shook his head. " She would n't go, old fellow. She 's in for a day's rest and odd jobs. I 'll tell you what, I 'll just drop round and let her know I 've found you, and then come back again. You 'll dine with us, won't you ? " Colonel Kenton had not always found old comradeship a bond between Mrs. Kenton and his friends, but he believed he could safely chance it with Davis, whom she had always rather liked, — with such small regard as a lady's devotion to her husband leaves her for his friends.

" Oh, I 'll *dine* with you fast enough," said his friend. " But why don't you send a note to Mrs. Kenton to say that we 'll be round together, and save yourself the bother ? Did you come here alone ? "

" Bless your heart, no ! I forgot him. The poor devil 's out there, cooling his heels on your stairs all this time. I came with a complete guide to Vienna. Can't you let him in out of the weather a minute ? "

" We 'll have him in, so that he can take your note

back; but he does n't expect to be decently treated:
they don't, here. You just sit down and write it,"
said the consul, pushing the colonel into his own
chair before his desk; and when the colonel had
superscribed his note, he called in the *Lohndiener*, —
patient, hat in hand, — and, "Where are you stopping?" he asked the colonel.

"Oh, I forgot that. At the Kaiserin Elisabeth.
I 'll just write it " —

"Never mind; we 'll tell him where to take it.
See here," added the consul in a serviceable Viennese
German of his own construction. "Take this to the
Kaiserin Elisabeth, quick;" and as the man looked up
in a dull surprise, "Do you hear? The Kaiserin
Elisabeth!"

"*I* don't know what it is about that hotel," said
the colonel, when the man had meekly bowed himself away, with a hat that swept the ground in honor
of a handsome drink-money; "but the mention of it
always seems to awaken some sort of reluctance in
the minds of the lower classes. Our driver wanted to
enter into conversation with me about it this morning at three o'clock, and I had to be pretty short with
him. If you don't know the language, it is n't so
difficult to be short in German as I 've heard. And
another curious thing is that Bradshaw says the

Kaiserin Elisabeth has a table d'hôte, and the head-waiter says she has n't, and never did have."

"Oh, you can't trust anybody in Europe," said the consul sententiously. "I'd leave Bradshaw and the waiter to fight it out among themselves. We'll get back in time to order a dinner; it's always better, and then we can dine alone, and have a good time."

"They could n't keep us from having a good time at a table d'hôte, even. But I don't mind."

By this time they had got on their hats and coats and sallied forth. They first went to a café and had some of that famous Viennese coffee; and then they went to the imperial and municipal arsenals, and viewed those collections of historical bricabrac, including the head of the unhappy Turkish general who was strangled by his sovereign because he failed to take Vienna in 1683. This from familiarity had no longer any effect upon the consul, but it gave Colonel Kenton prolonged pause. "I should have preferred a subordinate position in the sultan's army, I believe," he said. "Why, Davis, what a museum we could have had out of the Army of the Potomac alone, if Lincoln had been as particular as that sultan!"

From the arsenals they went to visit the parade-ground of the garrison, and came in time to see a manœuvre of the troops, at which they looked with

the frank respect and reserved superiority with which
our veterans seem to regard the military of Europe.
Then they walked about and noted the principal
monuments of the city, and strolled along the promenades and looked at the handsome officers and the
beautiful women. Colonel Kenton admired the life
and the gay movement everywhere; since leaving
Paris he had seen nothing so much like New York.
But he did not like their shovelling up the snow into
carts everywhere and dumping all that fine sleighing
into the Danube. "By the way," said his friend,
"let's go over into Leopoldstadt, and see if we can't
scare up a sleigh for a little turn in the suburbs."

"It's getting late, is n't it?" asked the colonel.

"Not so late as it looks. You know we have n't
the high American sun, here."

Colonel Kenton was having such a good time that
he felt no trouble about his wife, sitting over her
mending in the Kaiserin Elisabeth; and he yielded
joyfully, thinking how much she would like to hear
about the suburbs of Vienna: a husband will go
through almost any pleasure in order to give his wife
an entertaining account of it afterwards; besides, a
bachelor companionship is confusing: it makes many
things appear right and feasible which are perhaps
not so. It was not till their driver, who had turned

out of the beaten track into a wayside drift to make
room for another vehicle, attempted to regain the road
by too abrupt a movement, and the shafts of their
sledge responded with a loud crick-crack, that Colonel
Kenton perceived the error into which he had suffered
himself to be led. At three miles' distance from the
city, and with the winter twilight beginning to fall, he
felt the pang of a sudden remorse. It grew sorer with
every homeward step and with each successive failure to secure a conveyance for their return. In fine,
they trudged back to Leopoldstadt, where an absurd
series of discomfitures awaited them in their attempts
to get a fiacre over into the main city. They visited
all the stands known to the consul, and then they
were obliged to walk. But they were not tired, and
they made their distance so quickly that Colonel
Kenton's spirits rose again. He was able for the
first time to smile at their misadventure, and some
misgivings as to how Mrs. Kenton might stand affected towards a guest under the circumstances
yielded to the thought of how he should 'make her
laugh at them both. "Good old Davis!" mused the
colonel, and affectionately linked his arm through that
of his friend; and they stamped through the brilliantly
lighted streets gay with uniforms and the picturesque
costumes with which the Levant at Vienna encoun-

ters the London and Paris fashions. Suddenly the consul arrested their movement. "Did n't you say you were stopping at the Kaiserin Elisabeth ? "

"Why, yes ; certainly."

"Well, it 's just around the corner, here." The consul turned him about, and in another minute they walked under an archway into a court-yard, and were met by the portier at the door of his room with an inquiring obeisance.

Colonel Kenton started. The cap and the cap-band were the same, and it was to all intents and purposes the same portier who had bowed him away in the morning; but the face was different. On noting this fact Colonel Kenton observed so general a change in the appointments and even architecture of the place that, " Old fellow," he said to the consul, " you 've made a little mistake; this is n't the Kaiserin Elisabeth."

The consul referred the matter to the portier. Perfectly; that was the Kaiserin Elisabeth. " Well, then," said the colonel, "tell him to have us shown to my room." The portier discovered a certain embarrassment when the colonel's pleasure was made known to him, and ventured something in reply which made the consul smile.

" Look here, Kenton," he said, "*you 've* made a

little mistake, this time.   You 're not stopping at the
Kaiserin Elisabeth ! "

"Oh, pshaw !   Come now !   Don't bring the consular dignity so low as to enter into a practical joke
with a hotel porter.   It won't do.   We got into
Vienna this morning at three, and drove straight to
the Kaiserin Elisabeth.   We had a room and fire,
and breakfast about noon.   Tell him who I am, and
what I say."

The consul did so, the portier slowly and respectfully shaking his head at every point.   When it came
to the name, he turned to his books, and shook his
head yet more impressively.   Then he took down a
letter, spelled its address, and handed it to the
colonel ; it was his own note to Mrs. Kenton.   That
quite crushed him.   He looked at it in a dull, mechanical way, and nodded his head with compressed
lips.   Then he scanned the portier, and glanced round
once more at the bedevilled architecture.   " Well,"
said he, at last, " there 's a mistake somewhere.   Unless there are two Kaiserin Elisabeths —   Davis, ask
him if there are two Kaiserin Elisabeths."

The consul compassionately put the question, received with something like grief by the portier.   Impossible !

"Then I 'm not stopping at either of them," con-

tinued the colonel. " So far, so good, — if you want
to call it *good*. The question is now, if I'm not
stopping at the Kaiserin Elisabeth," he demanded,
with sudden heat, and raising his voice, " how the
devil did I get there ? "

The consul at this broke into a fit of laughter so
violent that the portier retired a pace or two from
these maniacs, and took up a safe position within his
doorway. " You did n't — you did n't — get there ! "
shrieked the consul. " That 's what made the whole
trouble. You — you meant well, but you got somewhere else." He took out his handkerchief and
wiped the tears from his eyes.

The colonel did not laugh ; he had no real pleasure
in the joke. On the contrary, he treated it as a
serious business. " Very well," said he, " it will be
proved next that I never told that driver to take me
to the Kaiserin Elisabeth, as it appears that I never
got there and am not. stopping there. Will you be
good enough to tell me," he asked, with polished sarcasm, " where I *am* stopping, and why, and how ? '

" I wish with all my heart I could," gasped his
friend, catching his breath, " but I can't, and the only
way is to go round to the principal hotels till we hit
the right one. It won't take long. Come ! " He
passed his arm through that of the colonel, and made

an explanation to the portier, as if accounting for the vagaries of some harmless eccentric he had in charge. Then he pulled his friend gently away, who yielded after a survey of .the portier and the court-yard with a frown in which an indignant sense of injury quite eclipsed his former bewilderment. He had still this defiant air when they came to the next hotel, and used the portier with so much severity on finding that he was not stopping there, either, that the consul was obliged to protest: " If you behave in that way, Kenton, I won't go with you. The man's perfectly innocent of your stopping at the wrong place; and some of these hotel people know me, and I won't stand your bullying them. And I tell you what: you 've got to let me have my laugh out, too. You know the thing 's perfectly ridiculous, and there 's no use putting any other face on it." The consul did not wait for leave to have his laugh out, but had it out in a series of furious gusts. At last the colonel himself joined him ruefully.

"Of course," said he, " I know I 'm an ass, and I would n't mind it on my own account. *I* would as soon roam round after that hotel the rest of the night as not, but I can't help feeling anxious about my wife. I 'm afraid she 'll be getting very uneasy at my being gone so long. She 's all alone, there, wherever it is, and —"

" Well, but she 's got your note. She 'll understand — "

" What a fool *you* are, Davis ! *There 's* my note ! "
cried the colonel, opening his fist and showing a very
small wad of paper in his palm. " She 'd have got
my note if she 'd been at the Kaiserin Elisabeth ; but
she 's no more there than I am."

" Oh ! " said his friend, sobered at this. " To be
sure ! Well ? "

" Well, it 's no use trying to tell a man like you ;
but I suppose that she 's simply distracted by this
time. You don't know what a woman is, and how
she can suffer about a little matter when she gives
her mind to it."

" Oh ! " said the consul again, very contritely.
" I 'm very sorry I laughed ; but " — here he looked
into the colonel's gloomy face with a countenance
contorted with agony — " this only makes it the more
ridiculous, you know ; " and he reeled away, drunk
with the mirth which filled him from head to foot.
But he repented again, and with a superhuman effort
so far subdued his transports as merely to quake in-
ternally, and tremble all over, as he led the way to
the next hotel, arm in arm with the bewildered and
embittered colonel. He encouraged the latter with
much genuine sympathy, and observed a proper

decorum in his interviews with one portier after another, formulating the colonel's story very neatly, and explaining at the close that this American Herr, who had arrived at Vienna before daylight and directed his driver to take him to the Kaiserin Elisabeth, and had left his hotel at one o'clock in the belief that it was the Kaiserin Elisabeth, felt now an added eagerness to know what his hotel really was from the circumstance that his wife was there quite alone and in probable distress at his long absence. At first Colonel Kenton took a lively interest in this statement of his case, and prompted the consul with various remarks and sub-statements; he was grateful for the compassion generally shown him by the portiers, and he strove with himself to give some account of the exterior and locality of his mysterious hotel. But the fact was that he had not so much as looked behind him when he quitted it, and knew nothing about its appearance; and gradually the reiteration of the points of his misadventure to one portier after another began to be as "a tale of little meaning, though the words are strong." His personation of an American Herr in great trouble of mind was an entire failure, except as illustrating the national apathy of countenance when under the influence of strong emotion. He ceased to take part in the con-

sul's efforts in his behalf; the whole abominable
affair seemed as far beyond his forecast or endeavor
as some result of malign enchantment, and there
was no such thing as carrying off the tragedy with
self-respect. Distressing as it was, there could be no
question but it was entirely ridiculous; he hung his
head with shame before the portiers at being a party
to it; he no longer felt like resenting Davis's amusement; he only wondered that he could keep his face
in relating the idiotic mischance. Each successive
failure to discover his lodging confirmed him in his
humiliation and despair. Very likely there was a
way out of the difficulty, but he did not know it.
He became at last almost an indifferent spectator of
the consul's perseverance. He began to look back
with incredulity at the period of his life passed before entering the fatal fiacre that morning. He
received the final portier's rejection with something
like a personal derision.

"That's the last place I can think of," said the
consul, wiping his brow as they emerged from the
court-yard, for he had grown very warm with walking
so much.

"Oh, all right," said the colonel languidly.

"But we won't give it up. Let's go in here and
get some coffee, and think it over a bit." They were

near one of the principal cafés, which was full of
people smoking, and drinking the Viennese *mélange*
out of tumblers.

" By all means," assented Colonel Kenton with
inconsequent courtliness, " think it over.   It 's all
that 's left us."

Matters did not look so dark, quite, after a tumbler
of coffee with milk, but they did not continue to
brighten so much as they ought with the cigars.
" Now let us go through the facts of the case," said
the consul, and the colonel wearily reproduced his
original narrative with every possible circumstance.
" But you know all about it," he concluded.   " I don't
see any end of it.   I don't see but I 'm to spend the
rest of my life in hunting up a hotel that professes
to be the Kaiserin Elisabeth, and is n't.   I never
knew anything like it."

" It certainly has the charm of novelty," gloomily
assented the consul : it must be owned that his gloom
was a respectful feint.   " I have heard of men running away from their hotels, but I never did hear
of a hotel running away from a man before now.
Yes — hold on ! I have, too.   Aladdin's palace —
and with Mrs. Aladdin in it, at that ! It 's a parallel
case." Here he abandoned himself as usual, while
Colonel Kenton viewed his mirth with a dreary grin.

When he at last caught his breath, " I beg your
pardon, I do, indeed," the consul implored. " I know
just how you feel, but of course it's coming out
right. We've been to all the hotels I know of, but
there must be others. We'll get some more names
and start at once ; and if the genie has dropped your
hotel anywhere this side of Africa we shall find it.
If the worst comes to the worst, you can stay at my
house to-night and start new to-m — Oh, I forgot !
— Mrs. Kenton ! Really, the whole thing is such an
amusing muddle that I can't seem to get over it."
He looked at Kenton with tears in his eyes, but con-
tained himself and decorously summoned a waiter,
who brought him whatever corresponds to a city di-
rectory in Vienna. " There !" he said, when he had
copied into his note-book a number of addresses, " I
don't think your hotel will escape us this time ;" and
discharging his account he led the way to the door,
Colonel Kenton listlessly following.

The wretched husband was now suffering all the
anguish of a just remorse, and the heartlessness of
his behavior in going off upon his own pleasure the
whole afternoon and leaving his wife alone in a
strange hotel to pass the time as she might was no
less a poignant reproach, because it seemed so incon-
ceivable in connection with what he had always

taken to be the kindness and unselfishness of his character. We all know the sensation; and I know none, on the whole, so disagreeable, so little flattering, so persistent when once it has established itself in the ill-doer's consciousness. To find out that you are not so good or generous or magnanimous as you thought is, next to having other people find it out, probably the unfriendliest discovery that can be made. But I suppose it has its uses. Colonel Kenton now saw the unhandsomeness of his leaving his wife at all, and he beheld in its true light his shabbiness in not going back to tell her he had found his old friend and was to bring him to dinner. The Lohndiener would of course have taken him straight to his hotel, and he would have been spared this shameful exposure, which, he knew well enough, Davis would never forget, but would tell all his life with an ever-increasing garniture of fiction. He cursed his weakness in allowing himself to dawdle about those arsenals and that parade-ground, and to be so far misguided by a hardened bachelor as to admire certain yellow-haired German and black-haired Hungarian women on the promenade; when he came to think of going out in that sledge, it was with anathema maranatha. He groaned in spirit, but he owned that he was rightly punished, though it seemed hard that his wife should be punished too. And then he went on miserably to figure first her slight surprise at his being gone so long; then her vague uneasiness and her conjectures; then her dawning apprehensions and her helplessness; her probable sending to the consulate to find out what had become of him; her dismay at learning nothing of him there; her waiting and waiting in wild dismay as the moments and hours went by; her frenzied running to the door at every step and her despair when it proved not his. He had seen her suffering from less causes. And where was she? In what low, shabby tavern had he left her? He choked with rage and grief, and could hardly speak to the gentleman, a naturalized fellow-citizen of Vienna, to whom he found the consul introducing him.

"I wonder if you can't help us," said the consul. "My friend here is the victim of a curious annoyance;" and he stated the case in language so sympathetic and decorous as to restore some small shreds of the colonel's self-respect.

"Ah," said their new acquaintance, who was mercifully not a man of humor, or too polite to seem so, "that's another trick of those scamps of fiacre-drivers. He took you purposely to the wrong hotel, and was probably feed by the landlord for bringing you. But why should you make yourselves so much trouble ? You know Colonel Kenton's landlord had to send his name to the police as soon as he came, and you can get his address there at once."

"Good-by !" said the consul very hastily, with a crestfallen air. "Come along, Kenton."

"What did he send my name to the police for ?" demanded the colonel, in the open air.

"Oh, it's a form. They do it with all travellers. It's merely to secure the imperial government against your machinations."

"And do you mean to say you ought to have known," cried the colonel, halting him, "that you could have found out where I was from the police at once, before we had walked all over this moral vineyard, and wasted half a precious lifetime ?"

"Kenton," contritely admitted the other, "I never happened to think of it."

"Well, Davis, you're a pretty consul !" That was all the colonel said, and though his friend was voluble in self-exculpation and condemnation, he did not answer him a word till they arrived at the police office. A few brief questions and replies between the commissary and the consul solved the long mystery, and Colonel Kenton had once more a hotel over

his head. The commissary certified to the respectability of the place, but invited the colonel to prose-
cute the driver of the fiacre in behalf of the general
public, — which seemed so right a thing that the
colonel entered into it with zeal, and then suddenly
relinquished it, remembering that he had not the
rogue's number, that he had not so much as looked at
him, and that he knew no more what manner of man
he was than his own image in a glass. Under the
circumstances, the commissary admitted that it was
impossible, and as to bringing the landlord to justice,
nothing could be proved against him.

"Will you ask him," said the colonel, "the outside
price of a first-class assault and battery in Vienna ? "

The consul put as much of this idea into German
as the language would contain, which was enough to
make the commissary laugh and shake his head
warningly.

"It would n't do, he says, Kenton; it is n't the
custom of the country."

"Very well, then, I don't see why we should
occupy his time." He gave his hand to the commissary, whom he would have liked to embrace, and
then hurried forth again with the consul. "There is
one little thing that worries me still," he said. "I
suppose Mrs. Kenton is simply crazy by this time."

" Is she of a very — nervous — disposition ? " faltered the consul.

" Nervous ? Well, if you could witness the expression of her emotions in regard to mice, you would n't ask that question, Davis."

At this desolating reply the consul was mute for a moment. Then he ventured : " I ' ve heard — or read, I don't know which — that women have more real fortitude than men, and that they find a kind of moral support in an actual emergency that they would n't find in — mice."

" Pshaw ! " answered the colonel. " You wait till you see Mrs. Kenton."

" Look here, Kenton," said the consul seriously, and stopping short. " I ' ve been thinking that perhaps — I — I had better dine with you some other day. The fact is, the situation now seems so purely domestic that a third person, you know — "

" Come along ! " cried the colonel. " I want you to help me out of this scrape. I ' m going to leave that hotel as soon as I can put my things together, and you ' ve got to browbeat the landlord for me while I go up and reassure my wife long enough to get her out of that den of thieves. What did you say the scoundrelly name was ? "

" The Gasthof zum Wilden Manne."

"And what does Wildun Manny mean?"

"The Sign of the Savage, we should make it, I suppose, — the Wild Man."

"Well, I don't know whether it was named after me or not; but if I 'd found that sign anywhere for the last four or five hours, I should have known it for home. There has n't been any wilder man in Vienna since the town was laid out, I reckon; and I don't believe there ever was a wilder woman anywhere than Mrs. Kenton is at this instant."

Arrived at the Sign of the Savage, Colonel Kenton left his friend below with the portier, and mounting the stairs three steps at a time flew to his room. Flinging open the door, he beheld his wife dressed in one of her best silks, before the mirror, bestowing some last prinks, touching her back hair with her hand and twitching the bow at her throat into perfect place. She smiled at him in the glass, and said, "Where 's Captain Davis?"

"Captain Davis?" gasped the colonel, dry-tongued with anxiety and fatigue. "Oh! *He 's* down there. He 'll be up directly."

She turned and came forward to him: "How do you like it?" Then she advanced near enough to encounter the moustache: "Why, how heated and tired you look!"

"Yes, yes, — we 've been walking.   I — I 'm rather late, ain't I, Bessie ? "

"About an hour.   I ordered dinner at six, and it 's nearly seven now."   The colonel started ; he had not dared to look at his watch, and he had supposed it must be about ten o'clock ; it seemed years since his search for the hotel had begun.   But he said nothing ; he felt that in some mysterious and unmerited manner Heaven was having mercy upon him, and he accepted the grace in the sneaking way we all accept mercy.   "I knew you 'd stay longer than you expected, when you found it was Davis."

"How did you know it was Davis ? " asked the colonel, blindly feeling his way.

Mrs. Kenton picked up her Almanach de Gotha. "It has all the consular and diplomatic corps in it."

"I won't laugh at it any more," said the colonel, humbly.   "Were n't you — uneasy, Bessie ? "

"No.   I mended away, here, and fussed round the whole afternoon, putting the trunks to rights ; and I got out this dress and ran a bit of lace into the collar ; and then I ordered dinner, for I knew you 'd bring the captain ; and I took a nap, and by that it was nearly dinner-time."

"Oh ! " said the colonel.

"Yes; and the head-waiter was as polite as peas; they've all been very attentive. I shall certainly recommend everybody to the Kaiserin Elisabeth."

"Yes," assented the wretched man. "I reckon it's about the best hotel in Vienna."

"Well, now, go and get Captain Davis. You can bring him right in here; we're only travellers. Why, what makes you act so queerly? Has anything happened?" Mrs. Kenton was surprised to find herself gathered into her husband's arms and embraced with a rapture for which she could see no particular reason.

"Bessie," said her husband, "I told you this morning that you were amiable as well as bright and beautiful; I now wish to add that you are sensible. I'm awfully ashamed of being gone so long. But the fact is we had a little accident. Our sleigh broke down out in the country, and we had to walk back."

"Oh, you poor old fellow! No wonder you look tired."

He accepted the balm of her compassion like a candid and innocent man: "Yes, it was pretty rough. But *I* didn't mind it, except on your account. I thought the delay would make you uneasy." With that he went out to the head of the stairs and called, "Davis!"

"Yes!" responded the consul; and he ascended the stairs in such trepidation that he tripped and fell part of the way up.

"Have you been saying anything to that man about my going away?"

"No, I've simply been blowing him up on the fiacre driver's account. He swears they are innocent of collusion. But of course they 're not."

"Well, all right. Mrs. Kenton is waiting for us to go to dinner. And look here," whispered the colonel, "don't you open your mouth, except to put something into it, till I give you the cue."

The dinner was charming, and had suffered little or nothing from the delay. Mrs. Kenton was in raptures with it, and after a thimbleful of the good Hungarian wine had attuned her tongue, she began to sing the praises of the Kaiserin Elisabeth.

"The K —" began the consul, who had hitherto guarded himself very well. But the colonel arrested him at that letter with a terrible look. He returned the look with a glance of intelligence, and resumed: "The Kaiserin Elisabeth has the best cook in Vienna."

"And everybody about has such nice, honest faces," said Mrs. Kenton. "I 'm sure I could n't have felt anxious if you had n't come till midnight: I knew I was perfectly secure here."

"Quite right, quite right," said the consul. "All classes of the Viennese are so faithful. Now, I dare say you could have trusted that driver of yours, who brought you here before daylight this morning, with untold gold. No stranger need fear any of the tricks ordinarily practised upon travellers in Vienna. They are a truthful, honest, virtuous population, — like all the Germans in fact."

"There, Ned! What do you say to that, with your Black Forest nonsense?" triumphed Mrs. Kenton.

Colonel Kenton laughed sheepishly : "Well, I take it all back, Bessie. I was n't quite satisfied with the appearance of the Black Forest country when I came to it," he explained to the consul, " and Mrs. Kenton and I had our little joke about the fraudulent nature of the Germans."

"*Our* little joke!" retorted his wife. " I wish we were going to stay longer in Vienna. They say you have to make bargains for everything in Italy, and here I suppose I could shop just as at home."

"Precisely," said the consul; the Viennese shop-keepers being the most notorious Jews in Europe.

"Oh, we can't stop longer than till the morning," remarked the colonel. "I shall be sorry to leave Vienna and the Kaiserin Elizabeth, but we must go."

"Better hang on awhile; you won't find many hotels like it, Kenton," observed his friend.

"No, I suppose not," sighed the colonel; "but I 'll get the address of their correspondent in Venice and stop there."

Thus these craven spirits combined to delude and deceive the helpless woman of whom half an hour before they had stood in such abject terror. If they had found her in hysterics they would have pitied and respected her; but her good sense, her amiability, and noble self-control subjected her to their shameless mockery.

Colonel Kenton followed the consul downstairs when he went away, and pretended to justify himself. "I 'll tell her one of these days," he said, "but there 's no use distressing her now."

"I did n't understand you at first," said the other. "But I see now it was the only way."

"Yes; saves needless suffering. I say, Davis, this is about an even thing between us? A United States consul ought to be of some use to his fellow-citizens abroad; and if he allows them to walk their legs off hunting up a hotel which he could have found at the first police-station if *he had happened to think of it*, he won't be very anxious to tell the joke, I suppose?"

"I don't propose to write home to the papers about it."

"All right." So, in the court-yard of the Wild Man, they parted.

Long after that Mrs. Kenton continued to recommend people to the Kaiserin Elisabeth. Even when the truth was made known to her she did not see much to laugh at. "I'm sure I was always very glad the colonel did n't tell me at once," she said, "for if I had known what I had been through, I certainly *should* have gone distracted."

TONELLI'S MARRIAGE.

TONELLI'S MARRIAGE.

THERE was no richer man in Venice than Tommaso Tonelli, who had enough on his florin a day; and none younger than he, who owned himself forty-seven years old. He led the cheerfullest life in the world, and was quite a monster of content; but when I come to sum up his pleasures, I fear that I shall appear to my readers to be celebrating a very insipid and monotonous existence. I doubt if even a summary of his duties could be made attractive to the conscientious imagination of hard-working people; for Tonelli's labors were not killing, nor, for that matter, were those of any Venetian that I ever knew. He had a stated employment in the office of the notary Cenarotti; and he passed there so much of every working day as lies between nine and five o'clock, writing upon deeds and conveyances and petitions and other legal instruments for the notary, who sat in an adjoining room, secluded from nearly everything in this world but snuff. He called Tonelli by the sound of a little bell; and, when he turned to take a paper from his safe, he seemed to be abstracting some secret from long-lapsed centuries, which he restored again, and locked back among the dead ages when his clerk replaced the document in his hands. These hands were very soft and pale, and their owner was a colorless old man, whose silvery hair fell down a face nearly as white ; but, as he has almost nothing to do with the present affair, I shall merely say that, having been compromised in the last revolution, he had been obliged to live ever since in perfect retirement, and that he seemed to have been blanched in this social darkness as a plant is blanched by growth in a cellar.   His enemies said that he was naturally a timid man, but they could not deny that he had seen things to make the brave afraid, or that he had now every reason from the police to be secret and cautious in his life.   He could hardly be called company for Tonelli, who must have found the day intolerably long but for the visit which the notary's pretty granddaughter contrived to pay every morning in the cheerless *mezzà*.   She commonly appeared on some errand from her mother, but her chief business seemed to be to share with Tonelli the modest feast of rumor and hearsay which he loved to furnish forth for her, and from which doubtless she carried back some fragments of gossip to the family apartments.

Tonelli called her, with that mingled archness and tenderness of the Venetians, his Paronsina; and, as he had seen her grow up from the smallest possible of Little Mistresses, there was no shyness between them, and they were fully privileged to each other's society by her mother. When she flitted away again, Tonelli was left to a stillness broken only by the soft breathing of the old man in the next room, and by the shrill discourse of his own loquacious pen, so that he was commonly glad enough when it came five o'clock. At this hour he put on his black coat, that shone with constant use, and his faithful silk hat, worn down to the pasteboard with assiduous brushing, and caught up a very jaunty cane in his hand. Then, saluting the notary, he took his way to the little restaurant, where it was his custom to dine, and had his tripe soup and his *risotto*, or dish of fried liver, in the austere silence imposed by the presence of a few poor Austrian captains and lieutenants. It was not that the Italians feared to be overheard by these enemies; but it was good *dimostrazione* to be silent before the oppressor, and not let him know that they even enjoyed their dinners well enough, under his government, to chat sociably over them. To tell the truth, this duty was an irksome one to Tonelli, who liked far better to dine, as he sometimes did, at a cook-shop, where he met the folk of the people (*gente del popolo*), as he called them; and where, though himself a person of civil condition, he discoursed freely with the other guests, and ate of their humble but relishing fare. He was known among them as Sior Tommaso; and they paid him a homage, which they enjoyed equally with him, as a person not only learned in the law, but a poet of gift enough to write wedding and funeral verses, and a veteran who had fought for the dead Republic of Forty-eight. They honored him as a most travelled gentleman, who had been in the Tyrol, and who could have spoken German, if he had not despised that tongue as the language of the ugly Croats, like one born to it. Who, for example, spoke Venetian more elegantly than Sior Tommaso? or Tuscan, when he chose? and yet he was poor, — a man of that genius! Patience! When Garibaldi came, we should see! The *facchini* and gondoliers, who had been wagging their tongues all day at the church corners and ferries, were never tired of talking of this gifted friend of theirs, when, having ended some impressive discourse or some dramatic story, he left them with a sudden adieu, and walked quickly away toward the Riva degli Schiavoni.

Here, whether he had dined at the cook-shop, or at

his more genteel and gloomy restaurant of the Bronze
Horses, it was his custom to lounge an hour or two
over a cup of coffee and a Virginia cigar at one of the
many caffès, and to watch all the world as it passed to
and fro on the quay. Tonelli was gray, he did not
disown it; but he always maintained that his heart
was still young, and that there was, moreover, a great
difference in persons as to age, which told in his
favor. So he loved to sit there, and look at the
ladies; and he amused himself by inventing a pet
name for every face he saw, which he used to teach
to certain friends of his, when they joined him over
his coffee. These friends were all young enough to
be his sons, and wise enough to be his fathers; but
they were always glad to be with him, for he had so
cheery a wit and so good a heart that neither his
years nor his follies could make any one sad. His
kind face beamed with smiles, when Pennellini, chief
among the youngsters in his affections, appeared on
the top of the nearest bridge, and thence descended
directly towards his little table. Then it was that he
drew out the straw which ran through the centre of
his long Virginia, and lighted the pleasant weed, and
gave himself up to the delight of making aloud those
comments on the ladies which he had hitherto stifled
in his breast. Sometimes he would feign himself too

deeply taken with a passing beauty to remain quiet, and would make his friend follow with him in chase of her to the Public Gardens. But he was a fickle lover, and wanted presently to get back to his caffè, where, at decent intervals of days or weeks, he would indulge himself in discovering a spy in some harmless stranger, who, in going out, looked curiously at the scar Tonelli's cheek had brought from the battle of Vicenza in 1848.

"Something of a spy, no?" he asked at these times of the waiter, who, flattered by the penetration of a frequenter of his caffè, and the implication that it was thought seditious enough to be watched by the police, assumed a pensive importance, and answered, "Something of a spy, certainly."

Upon this Tonelli was commonly encouraged to proceed: "Did I ever tell you how I once sent one of those ugly muzzles out of a caffè? I knew him as soon as I saw him, — I am never mistaken in a spy, — and I went with my newspaper, and sat down close at his side. Then I whispered to him across the sheet, 'We are two.' 'Eh?' says he. 'It is a very small caffè, and there is no need of more than one,' and then I stared at him and frowned. He looks at me fixedly a moment, then gathers up his hat and gloves, and takes his pestilency off."

The waiter, who had heard this story, man and boy, a hundred times, made a quite successful show of enjoying it, as he walked away with Tonelli's fee of half a cent in his pocket. Tonelli then had left from his day's salary enough to pay for the ice which he ate at ten o'clock, but which he would sometimes forego, in order to give the money in charity, though more commonly he indulged himself, and put off the beggar with, "Another time, my dear. I have no leisure now to discuss those matters with thee."

On holidays this routine of Tonelli's life was varied. In the forenoon he went to mass at St. Mark's, to see the beauty and fashion of the city; and then he took a walk with his four or five young friends, or went with them to play at bowls, or even made an excursion to the main land, where they hired a carriage, and all those Venetians got into it, like so many seamen, and drove the horse with as little mercy as if he had been a sail-boat. At seven o'clock Tonelli dined with the notary, next whom he sat at table, and for whom his quaint pleasantries had a zest that inspired the Paronsina and her mother to shout them into his dull ears, that he might lose none of them. He laughed a kind of faded laugh at them, and, rubbing his pale hands together, showed by his act that he did not think his best

wine too good for his kindly guest. The signora
feigned to take the same delight shown by her
father and daughter in Tonelli's drolleries; but I
doubt if she had a great sense of his humor, or, indeed, cared anything for it save as she perceived that
it gave pleasure to those she loved. Otherwise, however, she had a sincere regard for him, for he was
most useful and devoted to her in her quality of
widowed mother; and if she could not feel wit, she
could feel gratitude, which is perhaps the rarer gift,
if not the more respectable.

The Little Mistress was dependent upon him for
nearly all the pleasures and for the only excitements
of her life. As a young girl she was at best a sort
of caged bird, who had to be guarded against the
youth of the other sex as if they, on their part, were
so many marauding and ravening cats. During most
days of the year the Paronsina's parrot had almost as
much freedom as she. He could leave his gilded
prison when he chose, and promenade the notary's
house as far down as the marble well in the sunless
court, and the Paronsina could do little more. The
signora would as soon have thought of letting the
parrot walk across their campo alone as her daughter,
though the local dangers, either to bird or beauty,
could not have been very great. The green-grocer

of that sequestered campo was an old woman, the apothecary was gray, and his shop was haunted by none but superannuated physicians; the baker, the butcher, the waiters at the caffè were all professionally, and, as purveyors to her family, out of the question; the sacristan, who sometimes appeared at the perruquier's to get a coal from under the curling-tongs to kindle his censer, had but one eye, which he kept single to the service of the Church, and his perquisite of candle-drippings; and I hazard little in saying that the Paronsina might have danced a polka around Campo San Giuseppe without jeopardy so far as concerned the handsome wood-carver, for his wife always sat in the shop beside him. Nevertheless, a custom is not idly handed down by mother to daughter from the dawn of Christianity to the middle of the nineteenth century; and I cannot deny that the local perruquier, though stricken in years, was still so far kept fresh by the immortal youth of the wax heads in his window as to have something beauish about him; or that, just at the moment the Paronsina chanced to go into the campo alone, a *leone* from Florian's might not have been passing through it, when he would certainly have looked boldly at her, perhaps spoken to her, and possibly pounced at once upon her fluttering heart. So by day the Paronsina rarely went out, and she never emerged unattended from the silence and shadow of her grandfather's house.

If I were here telling a story of the Paronsina, or indeed any story at all, I might suffer myself to enlarge somewhat upon the daily order of her secluded life, and show how the seclusion of other Venetian girls was the widest liberty as compared with hers; but I have no right to play with the reader's patience in a performance that can promise no excitement of incident, no charm of invention. Let him figure to himself, if he will, the ancient and half-ruined palace in which the notary dwelt, with a gallery running along one side of its inner court, the slender pillars supporting upon the corroded sculpture of their capitals a clinging vine, that dappled the floor with palpitant light and shadow in the afternoon sun. The gate, whose exquisite Saracenic arch grew into a carven flame, was surmounted by the armorial bearings of a family that died of its sins against the Serenest Republic long ago ; the marble cistern which stood in the middle of the court had still a ducal rose upon either of its four sides ; and little lions of stone perched upon the posts at the head of the marble stairway climbing to the gallery, their fierce aspects worn smooth and amiable by the contact of

hands that for many ages had mouldered in tombs.
Toward the canal the palace windows had been im-
memorially bricked up for some reason or caprice,
and no morning sunlight, save such as shone from
the bright eyes of the Paronsina, ever looked into the
dim halls. It was a fit abode for such a man as the
notary, exiled in the heart of his native city, and it
was not unfriendly in its influences to a quiet vege-
tation like the signora's ; but to the Paronsina it was
sad as Venice itself, where, in some moods, I have
wondered that any sort of youth could have the courage to exist. Nevertheless, the Paronsina had contrived to grow up here a child of the gayest and
archest spirit, and to lead a life of due content, till
after her return home from the comparative freedom
and society of Madame Prateux's school, where she
spent three years in learning all polite accomplishments, and whence she came, with brilliant hopes and
romances ready imagined, for any possible exigency
of the future. She adored all the modern Italian
poets, and read their verse with that stately and
rhythmical fulness of voice which often made it sublime and always pleasing. She was a relentless pa-
triot, an Italianissima of the vividest green, white,
and red ; and she could interpret the historical novels
of her countrymen in their subtilest application to

the modern enemies of Italy. But all the Paronsina's gifts and accomplishments were to poor purpose, if they brought no young men a-wooing under
her balcony; and it was to no effect that her fervid
fancy peopled the palace's empty halls with stately
and gallant company out of Marco Visconti, Nicolò de'
Lapi, Margherita Pusterla, and the other romances,
since she could not hope to receive any practicable offer of marriage from the heroes thus assembled.
Her grandfather invited no guests of more substantial presence to his house. In fact, the police watched
him too narrowly to permit him to receive society,
even had he been so minded, and for kindred reasons
his family paid few visits in the city. To leave Venice, except for the autumnal *villeggiatura* was almost
out of the question; repeated applications at the
Luogotenenza won the two ladies but a tardy and
scanty grace; and the use of the passport allowing
them to spend a few weeks in Florence was attended
with so much vexation, in coming and going upon
the imperial confines, and when they returned
home they were subject to so great fear of perqui-
sition from the police, that it was after all rather
a mortification than a pleasure that the government
had given them. The signora received her few acquaintances once a week; but the Paronsina found

the old ladies tedious over their cups of coffee or tumblers of lemonade, and declared that her mamma's reception days were a martyrdom, — actually a martyrdom, to her. She was full of life and the beautiful and tender longing of youth; she had a warm heart and a sprightly wit; but she led an existence scarce livelier than a ghost's, and she was so poor in friends and resources that she shuddered to think what must become of her if Tonelli should die. It was not possible, thanks to God! that he should marry.

The signora herself seldom cared to go out, for the reason that it was too cold in winter and too hot in summer. In the one season she clung all day to her wadded arm-chair, with her *scaldino* in her lap; and in the other season she found it a sufficient diversion to sit in the great hall of the palace, and be fanned by the salt breeze that came from the Adriatic through the vine-garlanded gallery. But besides this habitual inclemency of the weather, which forbade out-door exercise nearly the whole year, it was a displeasure to walk in Venice on account of the stairways of the bridges; and the signora much preferred to wait till they went to the country in the autumn, when she always rode to take the air. The exceptions to her custom were formed by those after-dinner promenades which she sometimes made on holidays, in summer. Then she put on her richest black, and the Paronsina dressed herself in her best, and they both went to walk on the Molo, before the pillars of the lion and the saint, under the escort of Tonelli.

It often happened that, at the hour of their arrival on the Molo, the moon was coming up over the low bank of the Lido in the east, and all that prospect of ship-bordered quay, island, and lagoon, which, at its worst, is everything that heart can wish, was then at its best, and far beyond words to paint. On the right stretched the long Giudecca, with the domes and towers of its Palladian church, and the swelling foliage of its gardens, and its line of warehouses — painted pink, as if even Business, grateful to be tolerated amid such lovely scenes, had striven to adorn herself. In front lay San Giorgio, picturesque with its church and pathetic with its political prisons; and, farther away to the east again, the gloomy mass of the madhouse at San Servolo, and then the slender campanili of the Armenian convent rose over the gleaming and tremulous water. Tonelli took in the beauty of the scene with no more consciousness than a bird; but the Paronsina had learnt from her romantic poets and novelists to be complimentary to prospects, and her heart gurgled out in rapturous praises of this. The unwonted freedom exhilarated her; there was intoxication in the encounter of faces on the promenade, in the dazzle and glimmer of the lights, and even in the music of the Austrian band playing in the Piazza, as it came purified to her patriotic ear by the distance. There were none but Italians upon the Molo, and one might walk there without so much as touching an officer with the hem of one's garment; and, a little later, when the band ceased playing, she should go with the other Italians and possess the Piazza for one blessed hour. In the mean time, the Paronsina had a sharp little tongue; and, after she had flattered the landscape, and had, from her true heart, once for all, saluted the promenaders as brothers and sisters in Italy, she did not mind making fun of their peculiarities of dress and person. She was signally sarcastic upon such ladies as Tonelli chanced to admire, and often so stung him with her jests that he was glad when Pennellini appeared, as he always did exactly at nine o'clock, and joined the ladies in their promenade, asking and answering all those questions of ceremony which form Venetian greeting. He was a youth of the most methodical exactness in his whole life, and could no more have arrived on the Molo a moment before or

after nine than the bronze giants on the clock-tower
could have hastened or lingered in striking the hour.
Nature, which had made him thus punctual and precise, gave him also good looks, and a most amiable
kindness of heart. The Paronsina cared nothing at
all for him in his quality of handsome young fellow;
but she prized him as an acquaintance whom she
might salute, and be saluted by, in a city where her
grandfather's isolation kept her strange to nearly all
the faces she saw. Sometimes her evenings on the
Molo wasted away without the exchange of a word
save with Tonelli, for her mother seldom talked;
and then it was quite possible her teasing was greater
than his patience, and that he grew taciturn under
her tongue. At such times she hailed Pennellini's
appearance with a double delight; for, if he never
joined in her attacks upon Tonelli's favorites, he
always enjoyed them, and politely applauded them.
If his friend reproached him for this treason, he
made him every amend in answering, "She is jealous, Tonelli," — a wily compliment, which had the
most intense effect in coming from lips ordinarily so
sincere as his.

The signora was weary of the promenade long
before the Austrian music ceased in the Piazza, and
was very glad when it came time for them to leave

the Molo, and go and sit down to an ice at the Caffè
Florian.   This was the supreme hour to the Paronsina, the one heavenly excess of her restrained and
eventless life.   All about her were scattered tranquil
Italian idlers, listening to the music of the strolling
minstrels who had succeeded the military band ; on
either hand sat her friends, and she had thus the
image of that tender devotion without which a young
girl is said not to be perfectly happy ; while the very
heart of adventure seemed to bound in her exchange
of glances with a handsome foreigner at a neighbor-
ing table.   On the other side of the Piazza a few officers still lingered at the Caffè Quadri ; and at the
Specchi sundry groups of citizens in their dark dress
contrasted well with these white uniforms ; but, for
the most part, the moon and gas-jets shone upon the
broad, empty space of the Piazza, whose loneliness
the presence of a few belated promenaders only
served to render conspicuous.   As the giants ham-
mered eleven upon the great bell, the Austrian
sentinel, under the Ducal Palace, uttered a long,
reverberating cry ; and soon after a patrol of sol-
diers clanked across the Piazza, and passed with
echoing feet through the arcade into the narrow and
devious streets beyond.   The young girl found it
hard to rend herself from the dreamy pleasure of the

scene, or even to turn from the fine impersonal pain
which the presence of the Austrians in the spectacle
inflicted. All gave an impression something like that
of the theatre, with the advantage that here one's self
was part of the pantomime; and in those days, when
nearly everything but the puppet-shows was forbidden to patriots, it was altogether the greatest enjoy-
ment possible to the Paronsina. The pensive charm
of the place imbued all the little company so deeply
that they scarcely broke it, as they loitered slowly
homeward through the deserted Merceria. When
they reached the Campo San Salvatore, on many a
lovely summer's midnight, their footsteps seemed to
waken a nightingale whose cage hung from a lofty
balcony there; for suddenly, at their coming, the
bird broke into a wild and thrilling song, that touched
them all, and suffused the tender heart of the Paronsina with an inexpressible pathos.

Alas! she had so often returned thus from the
Piazza, and no stealthy footstep had followed hers
homeward with love's persistence and diffidence!
She was young, she knew, and she thought not
quite dull or hideous; but her spirit was as sole
in that melancholy city as if there were no youth
but hers in the world. And a little later than this,
when she had her first affair, it did not originate in

the Piazza, nor at all respond to her expectations
in a love-affair. In fact, it was altogether a business
affair, and was managed chiefly by Tonelli, who having met a young doctor, laurelled the year before at
Padua, had heard him express so pungent a curiosity
to know what the Paronsina would have to her
dower, that he perceived he must be madly in love
with her. So with the consent of the signora he had
arranged a correspondence between the young people;
and all went on well at first, — the letters from both
passing through his hands. But his office was anything but a sinecure, for while the Doctor was on his
part of a cold temperament, and disposed to regard
the affair merely as a proper way of providing for
the natural affections, the Paronsina cared nothing for
him personally, and only viewed him favorably as
abstract matrimony, — as the means of escaping from
the bondage of her girlhood and the sad seclusion of
her life into the world outside her grandfather's
house. So presently the correspondence fell almost
wholly upon Tonelli, who worked up to the point of
betrothal with an expense of finesse and sentiment
that would have made his fortune in diplomacy or
poetry. What should he say now? that stupid young
Doctor would cry in a desperation, when Tonelli deli-
cately reminded him that it was time to answer the

Paronsina's last note. Say this, that, and the other,
Tonelli would answer, giving him the heads of a
proper letter, which the Doctor took down on square
bits of paper, neatly fashioned for writing prescrip-
tions. " And for God's sake, caro dottore, put a little
warmth into it !" The poor Doctor would try, but it
must always end in Tonelli's suggesting and almost
dictating every sentence ; and then the letter, being
carried to the Paronsina made her laugh : " This is
very pretty, my poor Tonelli, but it was never my
onoratissimo dottore who thought of these tender compliments. Ah ! that allusion to my mouth and eyes
could only have come from the heart of a great poet.
It is yours, Tonelli, don't deny it." And Tonelli,
taken in his weak point of literature, could make but
a feeble pretence of disclaiming the child of his fancy,
while the Paronsina, being in this reckless humor,
more than once responded to the Doctor in such
fashion that in the end the inspiration of her altered
and amended letter was Tonelli's. Even after the
betrothal, the lovemaking languished, and the Doctor
was indecently patient of the late day fixed for the
marriage by the notary. In fact, the Doctor was very
busy; and, as his practice grew, the dower of the
Paronsina dwindled in his fancy, till one day he
treated the whole question of their marriage with

such coldness and uncertainty in his talk with Tonelli, that the latter saw whither his thoughts were
drifting, and went home with an indignant heart to
the Paronsina, who joyfully sat down and wrote her
first sincere letter to the Doctor, dismissing him.

"It is finished," she said, "and I am glad.   After
all, perhaps, I don't want to be any freer than I am ;
and while I have you, Tonelli, I don't want a younger
lover.   Younger ?   Diana !   You are in the flower of
youth, and I believe you will never wither.   Did
that rogue of a Doctor, then, really give you the elixir
of youth for writing him those letters ?   Tell me,
Tonelli, as a true friend, how long have you been
forty-seven ?   Ever since your fiftieth birthday ?
Listen !   I have been more afraid of losing you than
my sweetest Doctor.   I thought you would be so
much in love with lovemaking that you would go
break-neck and court some one in earnest on your
own account !"

Thus the Paronsina made a jest of the loss she had
sustained ; but it was not pleasant to her, except as it
dissolved a tie which love had done nothing to form.
Her life seemed colder and vaguer after it, and the
hour very far away when the handsome officers of her
king (all good Venetians in those days called Victor
Emanuel "our king") should come to drive out the

Austrians, and marry their victims. She scarcely enjoyed the prodigious privilege, offered her at this time in consideration of her bereavement, of going to the comedy, under Tonelli's protection and along with Pennellini and his sister, while the poor signora afterwards had real qualms of patriotism concerning the breach of public duty involved in this distraction of her daughter. She hoped that no one had recognized her at the theatre, otherwise they might have a warning from the Venetian Committee. " Thou knowest," she said to the Paronsina, " that they have even admonished the old Conte Tradonico, who loves the comedy better than his soul, and who used to go every evening.   Thy aunt told me, and that the old rogue, when people ask him why he does n't go to the play, answers, ' My mistress won't let me.'   But fie ! I am saying what young girls ought not to hear."

After the affair with the Doctor, I say, life refused to return exactly to its old expression, and I suppose that, if what presently happened was ever to happen, it could not have occurred at a more appropriate time for a disaster, or at a time when its victims were less able to bear it. I do not know whether I have yet sufficiently indicated the fact, but the truth is both the Paronsina and her mother had from long use come to regard Tonelli as a kind of property of theirs,

which had no right in any way to alienate itself.
They would have felt an attempt of this sort to be
not only very absurd, but very wicked, in view of
their affection for him and dependence upon him;
and while the Paronsina thanked God that he would
never marry, she had a deep conviction that he ought
not to marry, even if he desired. It was at the
same time perfectly natural, nay, filial, that she should
herself be ready to desert this old friend, whom she
felt so strictly bound to be faithful to her loneliness.
As matters fell out, she had herself primarily to
blame for Tonelli's loss; for, in that interval of disgust
and ennui following the Doctor's dismissal, she had
suffered him to seek his own pleasure on holiday
evenings; and he had thus wandered alone to the
Piazza, and so, one night, had seen a lady eating an
ice there, and fallen in love without more ado than
another man should drink a lemonade.

This facility came of habit, for Tonelli had now
been falling in love every other day for some forty
years; and in that time had broken the hearts of in-
numerable women of all nations and classes. The
prettiest water-carriers in his neighborhood were
in love with him, as their mothers had been before
them, and ladies of noble condition were believed
to cherish passions for him. Especially, gay and

beautiful foreigners, as they sat at Florian's, were
taken with hopeless love of him; and he could tell
stories of very romantic adventure in which he
figured as hero, though nearly always with moral
effect.   For example, there was the countess from the
mainland, — she merited the sad distinction of being
chief among those who had vainly loved him, if you
could believe the poet who both inspired and sang
her passion.   When she took a palace in Venice, he
had been summoned to her on the pretended business
of a secretary; but when she presented herself with
those idle accounts of her factor and tenants on the
mainland, her household expenses and her correspondence with her advocate, Tonelli perceived at
once that it was upon a wholly different affair that
she had desired to see him.   She was a rich widow of
forty, of a beauty supernaturally preserved and very
great.   "This is no place for thee, Tonelli mine," the
secretary had said to himself, after a week had passed,
and he had understood all the waywardness of that
unhappy lady's intentions.   "Thou art not too old, but
thou art too wise, for these follies, though no saint";
and so had gathered up his personal effects, and
secretly quitted the palace.   But such was the countess's fury at his escape that she never paid him his
week's salary; nor did she manifest the least gratitude

that Tonelli, out of regard for her son, a very honest
young man, refused in any way to identify her, but,
to all except his closest friends, pretended that he
had passed those terrible eight days on a visit to the
country village where he was born. It showed Pennellini's ignorance of life that he should laugh at this
history; and I prefer to treat it seriously, and to use
it in explaining the precipitation with which Tonelli's
latest inamorata returned his love.

Though, indeed, why should a lady of thirty, and
from an obscure country town, hesitate to be enamored of any eligible suitor who presented himself
in Venice? It is not my duty to enter upon a detail
or summary of Carlotta's character or condition, or to
do more than indicate that, while she did not greatly
excel in youth, good looks, or worldly gear, she had
yet a little property, and was of that soft prettiness
which is often more effective than downright beauty.
There was, indeed, something very charming about
her; and, if she was a blonde, I have no reason to
think she was as fickle as the Venetian proverb
paints that complexion of woman; or that she had
not every quality which would have excused any one
but Tonelli for thinking of marrying her.

After their first mute interview in the Piazza, the
two lost no time in making each other's acquaintance;

but though the affair was vigorously conducted, no
one could say that it was not perfectly in order.
Tonelli on the following day, which chanced to be
Sunday, repaired to St. Mark's at the hour of the
fashionable mass, where he gazed steadfastly at the
lady during her orisons, and whence, at a discreet distance, he followed her home to the house of the
friends whom she was visiting. Somewhat to his
discomfiture at first, these proved to be old acquaintances of his; and when he came at night to walk up
and down under their balconies, as bound in true love
to do, they made nothing of asking him indoors, and
presenting him to his lady. But the pair were not to
be entirely balked of their romance, and they still
arranged stolen interviews at church, where one
furtively whispered word had the value of whole
hours of unrestricted converse under the roof of their
friends. They quite refused to take advantage of
their anomalously easy relations, beyond inquiry on
his part as to the amount of the lady's dower, and on
hers as to the permanence of Tonelli's employment.
He in due form had Pennellini to his confidant, and
Carlotta unbosomed herself to her hostess; and the
affair was thus conducted with such secrecy that not
more than two thirds of Tonelli's acquaintance knew
anything about it when their engagement was announced.

There were now no circumstances to prevent their
early union, yet the happy conclusion was one to
which Tonelli urged himself after many secret and
bitter displeasures of spirit. I am persuaded that
his love for Carlotta must have been most ardent and
sincere, for there was everything in his history and
reason against marriage. He could not disown that
he had hitherto led a joyous and careless life, or that
he was exactly fitted for the modest delights, the discreet variety, of his present state, — for his daily
routine at the notary's, his dinner at the Bronze
Horses or the cook-shop, his hour at the caffè, his
walks and excursions, for his holiday banquet with
the Cenarotti, and his formal promenade with the
ladies of that family upon the Molo. He had a good
employment, with a salary that held him above want,
and afforded him the small luxuries already named;
and he had fixed habits of work and of relaxation,
which made both a blessing. He had his chosen
circle of intimate equals, who regarded him for his
good-heartedness and wit and foibles; and his little
following of humble admirers, who looked upon him
as a gifted man in disgrace with fortune. His friend-
ships were as old as they were secure and cordial; he
was established in the kindliness of all who knew
him; and he was flattered by the dependence of the

Paronsina and her mother, even when it was trouble-
some to him. He had his past of sentiment and war,
his present of story-telling and romance. He was
quite independent : his sins, if he had any, began and
ended in himself, for none was united to him so closely
as to be hurt by them ; and he was far too imprudent
a man to be taken for an example by any one. He
came and went as he listed, he did this or that without question. With no heart chosen yet from the
world of woman's love, he was still a young man, with
hopes and affections as pliable as a boy's. He had,
in a word, that reputation of good-fellow which in
Venice gives a man the title of *buon diavolo*, but on
which he does not anywhere turn his back with im-
punity, either from his own consciousness or from
public opinion. There never was such a thing in the
world as both good devil and good husband ; and even
with his betrothal Tonelli felt that his old, careless,
merry life of the hour ended, and that he had tacitly
recognized a future while he was yet unable to cut
the past. If one has for twenty years made a jest of
women, however amiably and insincerely, one does
not propose to marry a woman without making a jest
of one's self. The avenging remembrance of elderly
people whose late matrimony had furnished food for
Tonelli's wit now rose up to torment him, and in his

morbid fancy the merriment he had caused was echoed back in his own derision.

It shocked him to find how quickly his secret took wing, and it annoyed him that all his acquaintances were so prompt to felicitate him. He imagined a latent mockery in their speeches, and he took them with an argumentative solemnity. He reasoned separately with his friends; to all who spoke to him of his marriage he presented elaborate proofs that it was the wisest thing he could possibly do, and tried to give the affair a cold air of prudence. " You see, I am getting old; that is to say, I am tired of this bachelor life in which I have no one to take care of me, if I fall sick, and to watch that the doctors do not put me to death. My pay is very little, but, with Carlotta's dower well invested, we shall both together live better than either of us lives alone. She is a careful woman, and will keep me neat and comfortable. She is not so young as some women I had thought to marry, — no, but so much the better; nobody will think her half so charming as I do, and at my time of life that is a great point gained. She is good, and has an admirable disposition. She is not spoiled by Venice, but as innocent as a dove. O, I shall find myself very well with her ! "

This was the speech which with slight modification

Tonelli made over and over again to all his friends but Pennellini. To him he unmasked, and said boldly that at last he was really in love; and being gently discouraged in what seemed his folly, and incredulously laughed at, he grew angry, and gave such proofs of his sincerity that Pennellini was convinced, and owned to himself, "This madman is actually enamored, — enamored like a cat! Patience! What will ever those Cenarotti say?"

In a little while poor Tonelli lost the philosophic mind with which he had at first received the congratulations of his friends, and, from reasoning with them, fell to resenting their good wishes. Very little things irritated him, and pleasantries which he had taken in excellent part, time out of mind, now raised his anger. His barber had for many years been in the habit of saying, as he applied the stick of fixature to Tonelli's mustache, and gave it a jaunty upward curl, "Now we will bestow that little dash of youthfulness"; and it both amazed and hurt him to have Tonelli respond with a fierce "Tsit!" and say that this jest was proper in its antiquity to the times of Romulus rather than our own period, and so go out of the shop without that "Adieu, old fellow," which he had never failed to give in twenty years. "Capperi!" said the barber, when he emerged from a pro-

found revery into which this outbreak had plunged
him, and in which he had remained holding the nose
of his next customer, and tweaking it to and fro in
the violence of his emotions, regardless of those
mumbled maledictions which the lather would not
permit the victim to articulate. "If Tonelli is so savage in his betrothal, we must wait for his marriage to
tame him. I am sorry. He was always such a good
devil."

But if many things annoyed Tonelli, there were
some that deeply wounded him, and chiefly the fact
that his betrothal seemed to have fixed an impassable
gulf of years between him and all those young men
whose company he loved so well. He had really a
boy's heart, and he had consorted with them because he felt himself nearer their age than his own.
Hitherto they had in no wise found his presence a
restraint. They had always laughed, and told their
loves, and spoken their young men's thoughts, and
made their young men's jokes, without fear or shame,
before the merry-hearted sage, who never offered good
advice, if indeed he ever dreamed that there was a
wiser philosophy than theirs. It had been as if he
were the youngest among them ; but now, in spite of
all that he or they could do, he seemed suddenly and
irretrievably aged. They looked at him strangely, as if

for the first time they saw that his mustache was gray, that his brow was not smooth like theirs, that there were crow's-feet at the corners of his kindly eyes. They could not phrase the vague feeling that haunted their hearts, or they would have said that Tonelli, in offering to marry, had voluntarily turned his back upon his youth; that love, which would only have brought a richer bloom to their age, had breathed away forever the autumnal blossom of his.

Something of this made itself felt in Tonelli's own consciousness, whenever he met them, and he soon grew to avoid these comrades of his youth. It was therefore after a purely accidental encounter with one of them, and as he was passing into the Campo Sant' Angelo, head down, and supporting himself with an inexplicable sense of infirmity upon the cane he was wont so jauntily to flourish, that he heard himself addressed with, " I say, master!" He looked up, and beheld the fat madman who patrols that campo, and who has the license of his affliction to utter insolences to whomsoever he will, leaning against the door of a tobacconist's shop, with his arms folded, and a lazy, mischievous smile loitering down on his greasy face. As he caught Tonelli's eye he nodded, "Eh! I have heard, master"; while the idlers of that neighborhood, who relished and repeated his incoherent pleasantries like the *mots* of some great diner-out, gathered near with expectant grins. Had Tonelli been altogether himself, as in other days, he would have been far too wise to answer, " What hast thou heard, poor animal ? "

"That you are going to take a mate when most birds think of flying away," said the madman. " Because it has been summer a long time with you, master, you think it will never be winter. Look out : the wolf does n't eat the season."

The poor fool in these words seemed to utter a public voice of disapprobation and derision ; and as the pitiless bystanders, who had many a time laughed with Tonelli, now laughed at him, joining in the applause which the madman himself led off, the miserable good devil walked away with a shiver, as if the weather had actually turned cold. It was not till he found himself in Carlotta's presence that the long summer appeared to return to him. Indeed, in her tenderness and his real love for her he won back all his youth again ; and he found it of a truer and sweeter quality than he had known even when his years were few, while the gay old-bachelor life he had long led seemed to him a period of miserable loneliness and decrepitude. Mirrored in her fond eyes, he saw himself alert and handsome ; and, since

for the time being they were to each other all the
world, we may be sure there was nothing in the world
then to vex or shame Tonelli.   The promises of the
future, too, seemed not improbable of fulfilment, for
they were not extravagant promises.   These people's
castle in the air was a house furnished from Carlotta's modest portion, and situated in a quarter of
the city not too far from the Piazza, and convenient
to a decent caffè, from which they could order a
lemonade or a cup of coffee for visitors.   Tonelli's
stipend was to pay the housekeeping, as well as the
minute wage of a servant-girl from the country; and
it was believed that they could save enough from
that, and a little of Carlotta's money at interest, to
go sometimes to the Malibran theatre or the Marion-
ette, or even make an excursion to the mainland
upon a holiday; but if they could not, it was certainly better Italianism to stay at home; and at least
they could always walk to the Public Gardens.   At
one time, religious differences threatened to cloud this
blissful vision of the future; but it was finally agreed
that Carlotta should go to mass and confession as
often as she liked, and should not tease Tonelli about
his soul; while he, on his part, was not to speak ill
of the pope except as a temporal prince, or of any of
the priesthood except of the Jesuits when in com-

pany, in order to show that marriage had not made him a *codino*. For the like reason, no change was to be made in his custom of praising Garibaldi and reviling the accursed Germans upon all safe occasions.

As Tonelli had nothing in the world but his salary and his slender wardrobe, Carlotta eagerly accepted the idea of a loss of family property during the revolution. Of Tonelli's scar she was as proud as Tonelli himself.

When she came to speak of the acquaintance of all those young men, it seemed again like a breath from the north to her betrothed; and he answered, with a sigh, that this was an affair that had already finished itself. "I have long thought them too boyish for me," he said, "and I shall keep none of them but Pennellini, who is even older than I, — who, I believe, was never born, but created middle-aged out of the dust of the earth, like Adam. He is not a good devil, but he has every good quality."

While he thus praised his friend, Tonelli was meditating a service, which when he asked it of Pennellini, had almost the effect to destroy their ancient amity. This was no less than the composition of those wedding-verses, without which, printed and exposed to view in all the shop-windows, no one in Venice feels himself adequately and truly married. Pennel-

lini had never willingly made a verse in his life; and
it was long before he understood Tonelli, when he
urged the delicate request. Then in vain he protested, recalcitrated. It was all an offence to Tonelli's morbid soul, already irritated by his friend's
obtuseness, and eager to turn even the reluctance of
nature into insult. He took his refusal for a sign
that he, too, deserted him; and must be called back,
after bidding Pennellini adieu, to hear the only
condition on which the accursed sonnet would be
furnished, namely, that it should not be signed Pennellini, but An Affectionate Friend. Never was sonnet
cost poet so great anguish as this : Pennellinj went at
it conscientiously as if it were a problem in math-
ematics; he refreshed his prosody, he turned over
Carrer, he toiled a whole night, and in due time
appeared as Tonelli's affectionate friend in all the
butchers' and bakers' windows. But it had been too
much to ask of him, and for a while he felt the shock
of Tonelli's unreason and excess so much that there
was a decided coolness between them.

This important particular arranged, little remained
for Tonelli to do but to come to that open understanding with the Paronsina and her mother which
he had long dreaded and avoided. He could not con-
ceal from himself that his marriage was a kind of de-

sertion of the two dear friends so dependent upon
his singleness, and he considered the case of the
Paronsina with a real remorse. If his meditated act
sometimes appeared to him a gross inconsistency and
a satire upon all his former life, he had still consoled
himself with the truth of his passion, and had found
love its own apology and comfort ; but in its relation
to these lonely women, his love itself had no fairer
aspect than that of treason, and he shrank from own-
ing it before them with a sense of guilt. Some wild
dreams of reconciling his future with his past occa-
sionally haunted him ; but in his saner moments, he
perceived their folly. Carlotta, he knew, was good
and patient, but she was nevertheless a woman, and
she would never consent that he should be to the
Cenarotti all that he had been ; these ladies also
were very kind and reasonable, but they too were
women, and incapable of accepting a less perfect devotion. Indeed, was not his proposed marriage too
much like taking her only son from the signora and
giving the Paronsina a stepmother ? It was worse,
and so the ladies of the notary's family viewed it,
cherishing a resentment that grew with Tonelli's delay to deal frankly with them ; while Carlotta, on
her part, was wounded that these old friends should
ignore his future wife so utterly. On both sides
evil was stored up.

When Tonelli would still make a show of fidelity
to the Paronsina and her mother, they accepted his
awkward advances, the latter with a cold visage, the
former with a sarcastic face and tongue. He had
managed particularly ill with the Paronsina, who,
having no romance of her own, would possibly have
come to enjoy the autumnal poetry of his love if he
had permitted. But when she first approached him
on the subject of those rumors she had heard, and
treated them with a natural derision, as involving the
most absurd and preposterous ideas, he, instead of
suffering her jests, and then turning her interest to
his favor, resented them, and closed his heart and
its secret against her. What could she do, thereafter,
but feign to avoid the subject, and adroitly touch it
with constant, invisible stings ? Alas! it did not
need that she should ever speak to Tonelli with the
wicked intent she did; at this time he would have
taken ill whatever most innocent thing she said.
When friends are to be estranged, they do not require
a cause. They have but to doubt one another, and
no forced forbearance or kindness between them can
do aught but confirm their alienation. This is on the
whole fortunate, for in this manner neither feels to
blame for the broken friendship, and each can declare
with perfect truth that he did all he could to main-

tain it. Tonelli said to himself, "If the Paronsina had treated the affair properly at first!" and the Paronsina thought, "If he had told me frankly about it to begin with!" Both had a latent heartache over their trouble, and both a sense of loss the more bitter because it was of loss still unacknowledged.

As the day fixed for Tonelli's wedding drew near, the rumor of it came to the Cenarotti from all their acquaintance. But when people spoke to them of it, as of something they must be fully and particularly informed of, the signora answered coldly, " It seems that we have not merited Tonelli's confidence " ; and the Paronsina received the gossip with an air of clearly affected surprise, and a *" Davvero ! "* that at least discomfited the tale-bearers.

The consciousness of the unworthy part he was acting toward these ladies had come at last to poison the pleasure of Tonelli's wooing, even in Carlotta's presence ; yet I suppose he would still have let his wedding-day come and go, and been married beyond hope of atonement, so loath was he to inflict upon himself and them the pain of an explanation, if one day, within a week of that time, the notary had not bade his clerk dine with him on the morrow. It was a holiday, and as Carlotta was at home, making ready for the marriage, Tonelli consented to take his place

at the table from which he had been a long time
absent. But it turned out such a frigid and melancholy banquet as never was known before. The old
notary, to whom all things came dimly, finally missed
the accustomed warmth of Tonelli's fun, and said,
with a little shiver, "Why, what ails you, Tonelli?
You are as moody as a man in love."

The notary had been told several times of Tonelli's
affair, but it was his characteristic not to remember
any gossip later than that of 'Forty-eight.

The Paronsina burst into a laugh full of the cruelty
and insult of a woman's long-smothered sense of injury. "Caro nonno," she screamed into her grandfather's dull ear, "he is really in despair how to
support his happiness. He is shy, even of his old
friends, — he has had so little experience. It is the
first love of a young man. Bisogna compatire la
gioventù, caro nonno." And her tongue being finally
loosed, the Paronsina broke into incoherent mockeries,
that hurt more from their purpose than their point,
and gave no one greater pain than herself.

Tonelli sat sad and perfectly mute under the inflic-
tion, but he said in his heart, "I have merited worse."

At first the signora remained quite aghast; but
when she collected herself, she called out peremp-
torily, "Madamigella, you push the affair a little
beyond. Cease!"

The Paronsina, having said all she desired, ceased, panting.

The old notary, for whose slow sense all but her first words had been too quick, though all had been spoken at him, said dryly, turning to Tonelli, "I imagine that my deafness is not always a misfortune."

It was by an inexplicable, but hardly less inevitable, violence to the inclinations of each that, after this miserable dinner, the signora, the Paronsina, and Tonelli should go forth together for their wonted promenade on the Molo. Use, which is the second, is also very often the stronger nature, and so these parted friends made a last show of union and harmony. In nothing had their amity been more fatally broken than in this careful homage to its forms; and now, as they walked up and down in the moonlight, they were of the saddest kind of apparitions, — not mere disembodied spirits, which, however, are bad enough, but disanimated bodies, which are far worse, and of which people are not more afraid only because they go about in society so commonly. As on many and many another night of summers past, the moon came up and stood over the Lido, striking far across the glittering lagoon, and everywhere winning the flattered eye to the dark masses of shadow upon the water; to the trees of the Gardens, to the

trees and towers and domes of the cloistered and
templed isles.   Scene of pensive and incomparable
loveliness! giving even to the stranger, in some faint
and most unequal fashion, a sense of the awful meaning of exile to the Venetian, who in all other lands
in the world is doubly an alien, from their unuttera-
ble unlikeness to his sole and beautiful city.   The
prospect had that pathetic unreality to the friends
which natural things always assume to people playing a part, and I imagine that they saw it not more
substantial than it appears to the exile in his dreams.
In their promenade they met again and again the
unknown, wonted faces; they even encountered some
acquaintances, whom they greeted, and with whom
they chatted for a while; and when at nine the
bronze giants beat the hour upon their bell, — with
as remote effect as if they were giants of the times
before the flood, — they were aware of Pennellini,
promptly appearing like an exact and methodical
spectre.

But to-night the Paronsina, who had made the
scene no compliments, did not insist as usual upon
the ice at Florian's; and Pennellini took his formal
leave of the friends under the arch of the Clock
Tower, and they walked silently homeward through
the echoing Merceria.

At the notary's gate Tonelli would have said good-night, but the signora made him enter with them, and then abruptly left him standing with the Paronsina in the gallery, while she was heard hurrying away to her own apartment. She reappeared, extending toward Tonelli both hands, upon which glittered and glittered manifold skeins of the delicate chain of Venice.

She had a very stately and impressive bearing, as she stood there in the moonlight, and addressed him with a collected voice. "Tonelli," she said, "I think you have treated your oldest and best friends very cruelly. Was it not enough that you should take yourself from us, but you must also forbid our hearts to follow you even in sympathy and good wishes? I had almost thought to say adieu forever to-night; but," she continued, with a breaking utterance, and passing tenderly to the familiar form of address, "I cannot part so with thee. Thou hast been too like a son to me, too like a brother to my poor Clarice. Maybe thou no longer lovest us, yet I think thou wilt not disdain this gift for thy wife. Take it, Tonelli, if not for our sake, perhaps then for the sake of sorrows that in times past we have shared together in this unhappy Venice."

Here the signora ended perforce the speech, which

had been long for her, and the Paronsina burst into
a passion of weeping, — not more at her mamma's
words than out of self-pity and from the national
sensibility.

Tonelli took the chain, and reverently kissed it
and the hands that gave it. He had a helpless sense
of the injustice the signora's words and the Paronsina's tears did him; he knew that they put him
with feminine excess further in the wrong than even
his own weakness had; but he tried to express nothing of this, — it was but part of the miserable maze
in which his life was involved. With what courage
he might he owned his error, but protested his faithful friendship, and poured out all his troubles, — his
love for Carlotta, his regret for them, his shame and
remorse for himself. They forgave him, and there
was everything in their words and will to restore
their old friendship, and keep it; and when the gate
with a loud clang closed upon Tonelli, going from
them, they all felt that it had irrevocably perished.

I do not say that there was not always a decent
and affectionate bearing on the part of the Paronsina
and her mother towards Tonelli and his wife; I
acknowledge that it was but too careful and faultless
a tenderness, ever conscious of its own fragility. Far
more natural was the satisfaction they took in the

delayed fruitfulness of Tonelli's marriage, and then in the fact that his child was a girl, and not a boy. It was but human that they should doubt his happiness, and that the signora should always say, when hard pressed with questions upon the matter: "Yes, Tonelli is married; but if it were to do again, I think he would do it to-morrow rather than to-day."

THE END.